Autograph Album

AUTOGRAPH ALBUM

Theodore Dawes

New American Society for Historical Research
New England Monographs   1

Laboratory Books
Astoria, Queens

The New American Society for Historical Research (NASHR) is dedicated to the growth of knowledge beyond those rigid, artificial boundaries enforced by academic gatekeepers.

Learn more at newamericansociety.org.

Frontispiece: Front cover of Annie McFarlane's autograph album, actual size

Laboratory Books LLC
35-19 31st Avenue, No. 4R
Astoria, NY 11106
www.laboratorybooks.xyz

First edition
10 9 8 7 6 5 4 3 2 1

ISBN 978-1-946053-14-5

Library of Congress Control Number: 2020933601

Text set in Clarendon URW, Freight Sans, Freight Text

Printed in China

Contents

. . . but we, at haphazard
And unseasonably, are brought face to face
By ones, Clio, with your silence. . . .
　　　—W. H. Auden, "Homage to Clio"

Introduction

The autograph album herein reproduced belonged to Anne McFarlane Dawes, or "Annie," my paternal great-grandmother. Compiled between 1888 and 1889—her fifteenth and sixteenth years, more or less—the album consists of a rectangular block of sturdy paper, well-yellowed and smelling of mildew, bound by cloth covers that leave, nowadays, a difficult residue on one's fingertips. Purchased from a dime store, I suppose, or from a neighborhood stationer's, along with the sort of fat, stubby pencil one must sharpen with a knife. I have no articles recording the fact of it—no receipts, no parallel diaries. It hardly matters. I confess that an autograph book strikes me as a dull pastime; nevertheless, Victorian girls of the literate classes adored a good autograph, apparently, every bit as much as they adored a marriage plot, or a well-played hand of bridge.

Annie was born on June 14, 1873, in her family home in Roslindale, Massachusetts (now divided into four rent-stabilized apartments), and died on October 8, 1966, at Silver Hill Memorial Hospital in Framingham, and while that span encompasses much history, much progress, I regret to report that she lacked the temperament to appreciate, or even consider, context. Of greater concern was the timeliness of her supper, tax rates and the cost of milk (always upsetting), and the new families degrading her neighborhood. Her occasional journals record only air temperature and the demographics of birds. My father recalls, from his young visits, her disgusting perfume—like lilacs and spoiled meat, he says—and the bowed sashes of her perpetually drawn curtains. She wore black or navy skirts with their hems at her ankles. She placed lace cloths beneath every lamp and candy dish. She considered jam *and* butter, together, a ruinous decadence. She exhibited a great tolerance of physical discomfort: she set her own broken wrist, pulled her own spoiled tooth, and six days before she died her radiologist discovered blooming from her liver a tumor the size of a baseball glove, of which no symptoms had ever been disclosed. I, of course, never met the dotty crow—she was a decade dead before a potential me first interfered with my parents' predictive organs (which, by the way, I have determined, through extensive self-contemplation and the analysis of suppressed literature, do not reside in the brain—but there's a future book). My gracious, though, do I know her—she, or rather her emblematic type, is an essential feature of the New England landscape, as much as a mill dam, a glaciated hillock, or some boggy pond with a Wampanoag name.

We must thank my father, Edward Arthur Dawes, for the existence of this book: thanks, Dad. Following his retirement from Reinhardt Srinivasan LLP, the Cambridge firm he scrupulously served as Director of Accounting, Dad got it in mind to move to the vacation property he'd purchased for its passive rental income, a silly Alpine-styled chalet on acreage at Jackson Hole—this despite having dismissed, all his life, as irremediably wretched all territory west of the Hudson River. Dad's never skied in his life—hates skiers, in fact, almost as much as he does cyclists—and yet there he abides, with his views of gondolas and snowy slopes. He now mentions with grim satisfaction how many square feet of brush he can clear on a sunny afternoon, and he owns a plaid shirt with twin pockets and pearl buttons, and he has gone for drinks with women named Connie and Lynette—but I digress. While emptying his Massachusetts house for the market—my childhood home, a rambling beast in the Federal style, goldenrod clapboards with ornate white trim, roses in summer, apples in autumn—Dad found, in his sodden cellar, an antique steamer trunk, at the bottom of which, beneath layers of mauled afghans and stained silk curtains, Annie's album lay, wrapped in oilcloth. The trunk had passed from family household to family household for generations—Dad took it from his own father's home, when the old man's dementia at last required his forcible commitment to Willowbrook Manor—rarely displayed, rarely opened, a pointless cycle that I took it upon myself to break: it is now in the possession of a West Brimfield dealer in antiquities whose six hundred cash dollars are in a windowed business envelope somewhere or other among my effects, likely in an interior chamber of my attaché. Dad doesn't understand this project, by the way. "I'd say you were squandering your legacy," he's said, "if you hadn't already done so." I don't know whether he's concerned with the state of my trust or of my good name. Either way, these are not conversations I suffer to continue. It's difficult to have a serious exchange with a man whom I suspect is wearing a Stetson.

Here is as fine a point as any for me to express my total absence of gratitude—its vacant spot is as black and airless as intergalactic void—to the State Historical Society of Massachusetts. My intention had been to make extensive use of their archives—indeed, my initial plan for this work relied upon this. I anticipated fruitful days spent in the plush reading room of the society's headquarters, perusing old correspondence and indexes of voters and examining photographs with a loupe, interspersed with restful moments leaning on a windowsill, overlooking a well-groomed quadrangle and swan-dense reflecting pool, all in an atmosphere of mahogany paneling, velvet drapes, brass lamps with banker's shades. Alas, Dr. Jeremy Lawson, the unctuous monkey with whom I met at the society's Central Square office—a rented space above a kebab shop, all polyester carpet and nictitating fluorescence—dashed any hope of such a civilized engagement. Lawson sat with a fixed fake smile, air whistling through his thicket of nose hairs, as I gave my prepared speech and taped to his whiteboard my professionally printed charts. A loose joint in his rolling chair whined. He cocked his head. He appeared to make notes with his inexpensive ballpoint—I realized later that these were cartoon faces and spiral doodles. My dismissal was brief and graceless. In another era I would have struck his slick pink cheek with my riding glove, and in the morning Lawson's second would be dragging his corpse across some dewy meadow, toward the opened trunk of the hearse I had presciently summoned. "Credentials." "Accreditation." These are the refuges of tiny minds—sealed chambers into which they might retreat when confronted by an invasion of such fierce talents as they could never dream to possess. Let them hoard their sad trove. Let them rot among their antique shoe buckles and pepper pots. Intelligence is its own research, and I am nothing if not intelligent; truth is lovelier than fact, and truth is a resource of which I have discovered a rich, unworked seam, subject to no prior claim. (One not distant day, when my present leisure has grown stale, I'll establish a parallel society, dedicated to the independent researcher, not subject to petty politics, jealousy, sociological trends, or personal vendettas—only to knowledge as undiluted as arctic snow. I desire no more than to arrange an apparatus of funding—though when the board comes seeking its chairman, there will be no one with more relevant experience, or a more personal stake in the society's success, than I. The burden of the gavel is one I will suffer in the name of a noble cause. Prizes awarded. Portraits painted. Refreshments served.)

Nevertheless, my work is complete. I drove thousands of miles in rented cars. I braved the unchanged beds of backwoods lodges, and supped on clotted grease in filthy, fly-haunted cafés. I spoke to seniles. I spoke to morons. I tolerated halitosis and shook unwashed hands. I read postcards and census books, ledgers and telephone directories. I wore two boxes of Ticonderogas down to their chewed ferrules, and lost a third. Though I've never been a swimmer, a boater, a lover of the outdoors, I feel, in this exceptional moment—the crowning, here, of my creation, of all my excellent work—the lure of the ocean, and I long to see the yolk of the sun go boiling on its horizon. A fellow likes now a pinch of primordial awe, like salt on his sirloin. Eight blocks away from my current rooms, on the far side of the tourist cottages and mock-hacienda hotels, the tiled pools and florid bougainvillea, the taco trucks and margarita bars, that constitute this lurid town, whose tourist brochures misled me as to its virtues—I had an impression of fog-shrouded mornings, a fireside writing desk, and long twilights silent save for the barking of seals—is the beach. I will walk the length of Seaview Avenue, scoffing at the panhandlers, with their scarred dogs and three-stringed guitars and patched canvas coats, elbowing past all the plump touring men in deck shoes and long short pants with many pockets, the puffed, injected ladies with their kidney-sized purses and wax-handled shopping bags overstuffed with boxes of taffy and novelty T-shirts, past the rampant, repellent children with their oozing cones of soft serve and abundant disease. These are the carved devils that line the processional road to paradise, to the temple of the sparkling mind, erected to ward one and to warn one against worldliness, and against all those petty, ancillary realities that to acknowledge would mean to diminish one's own. At the Dolphin Market, adjacent to the beachfront, I will purchase a lush young cabernet—the vintner, with whom I have, over the course of my visits to his premises, formed a little society of mutual admiration, grows his grapes on a hillside five miles north, overlooking the coastal highway, and has promised to prepare for me a stuffed game hen in exchange for an autographed copy of this volume—and a wax Coca-Cola cup in which to decant it. At the lip of the sea I will lay my plaid quilt on black sand and sit upon it, crossing my legs like a guru. I will sip my wine and contemplate the boundless Pacific, my rigid back facing ever East.

Theodore Dawes
Tocon Del Mar, California
November 17, 2019

The Autograph Album

Andrew McFarlane was born to an Irish laborer and his washer wife—a filthy pair of famine refugees from Leitrim. Raised amid the brothels, synagogues, and labor halls of Boston's mercifully razed West End, Andrew left school after grade eight to work the varied odd jobs required of boys in capitalist mythology: newspaper hawker, flower seller, horse groom, boiler attendant, brevet corporal, lawyer's page, debt collector, et cetera. He would have kept this up, and kept frequenting his favorite cabarets and iniquitous dens, until he acquired syphilis and a distended liver and was exiled to the Indian Territory, or drowned in a millpond—whatever they did with such beasts of appetite as he—had he not been besotted by Mary MacLeod, a schoolteacher he met in the Public Garden, on the swan boats. He knocked her up, they wed; he was set up in business by Mary's father, an upright Scot with lips like an anus who had done well in the linen trade; and Andrew took to bourgeois splendor like an iguana to the blaze of its heat lamp.

Profligate, boisterous, autodidactic, fiercely bearded, charming to ladies, kind to paupers, fond of song, fond of carousing, Andrew was detested by my paternal great-great-grandfather, Capt. Abraham Dawes, who preferred to spend his free hours reading at the Athenæum

When the leaves of this, though faded with age,
May cause you to look, through memories tears
We'll brush them away, a moment to see,
The lines that your "Father" has written for the

Your Father,

Boston Mass

Andrew Mc Farlan
Mar 9th 1889

or sipping gin in his club's drawing room, and whose nape-hair never brushed his collar. Nevertheless, they became housemates in late life, following their synchronized widowhoods, at the insistence of their children, who found them intolerable boarders. They inhabited a rented Queen Anne cottage in West Roxbury. Abraham complained in letters to his son—that is, my great-grandfather, Mr. Annie McFarlane, Charles P. Dawes—of abundant flatulence, and obscene piano rolls, and the perfumed girls with vulgar accents whom Andrew bundled up the back staircase. Yet the pair proved inseparable, bickering about politics and poetry on garden benches while they fed almonds to tame squirrels, sharing their preferred journals, dining Wednesday and Friday evenings at the Parker House.

Andrew died in 1919—that epidemic, I suppose, or grotesque age. At the funeral Abraham spat into the open grave, a gluey gob among the casket's massed lilies; neat mustache twitching, hands clasping heart as his sons restrained him, he declared it an act that the late Andrew would damned well understand. As Abraham stalked back to his waiting carriage, he speared and eviscerated with the tip of his umbrella all the crocuses abloom along the cobbled footpath.

[2r, loose]

Bosto[. . .]y 25th 188[. . .]

When twilight draws her curtain
and pins it with a star
will you sometimes think of me
though I may wander far,

Chas. Broussard
Cambrigeport
Mass

Not to be confused with the Broussards of Prospect Street (a clot of dyspeptic Acadians—costermongers, charwomen, accordionists, and drunks), the Cambridgeport Broussards were a respectable family, though Catholic. They had been wealthy, holding in trust productive properties throughout the Carolinas, but this fortune was undone, alas, by the Civil War. The privations were nobly suffered, and the previous generation's exquisite manners were retained. Mr. Broussard tutored in Latin and Greek, and wrote pithy essays for the Sunday papers. Mrs. Broussard was a direct descendant of Lord Baltimore. I can't imagine how they came to associate with such petit bourgeois climbers as the McFarlanes. I suppose they were very kind, or very polite.

Charles's glib note should not be taken to indicate ardor. Seventeen already, he began at Harvard that autumn, acquiring tastes for sherry and the facetious banter of toffs. He rowed crew, mastered the classics, made the A.D. Club, indulged in Scollay Square fancy houses, and went most Saturdays shooting quail with his roommate, a Roosevelt. Upon graduation Charles took a position in the Department of State. The nature of his portfolio there is unclear; he claimed to spend most of his day reading adventure magazines in his office and

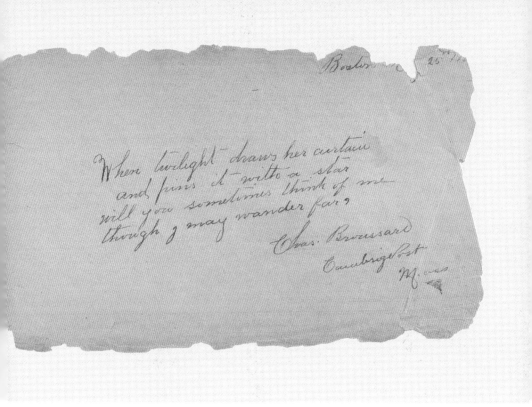

applying to reports his occasional certifying stamp. He was even less forthcoming about his foreign missions—one's inquiries received no more than a helpless shrug—but he always returned with amusing souvenirs: a set of erotic matryoshka dolls, congas painted with the face of King Alfonso.

Charles's marriage to a Georgetown widow seven years his senior aroused some consternation among his relations and his superiors—this woman, Ida, possessed an indecently sensual comportment and, it must be said, a rather Hebraic profile—but she dressed so well, and had several millions from her late husband. Charles's parents found Ida less upsetting than his mercenary embrace of Episcopalianism. The couple's sole issue, a daughter called Eunice, was feebleminded and died of a blood infection, aged fourteen years, in 1910; Charles himself died a month later beneath the wheels of the Penn Colonial. His discreet funeral was attended by Secretary Knox and two Rockefellers. President Taft dispatched a tender card.

What an awful flower.

You would be surprised—or perhaps you wouldn't: I don't pretend to know you, reader—how common was the name "Jennie MacDonald" in the late nineteenth century. I had assumed—an unwarranted assumption, yes—that "Jennifer" (such a frivolous name) was deployed but rarely before the 1950s, and certainly not by families of staid Scottish shopkeepers. I would expect such to bestow on their offspring sturdier things: Agatha, Agnes. Broad-hipped, big-calved names. Names evoking calloused palms, twin beds, thin sheets, hidden liquor, hand-me-downs, and floral kerchiefs; an inability to allow maids and cooks and custodians to perform their duties without interference; rationed salt and pepper; tinned milk; and whisk brooms, hideous whisk brooms. But I know so little, the fact of which everything conspires to remind me.

This particular Jennie MacDonald was Annie McFarlane's maternal second cousin. A gaunt girl with hair so flat and limp that she appeared always to have just come inside from the rain, Jennie married a Dr. Charles Brodie of Quincy, excreted offspring, moved to a splendid house, cultivated roses, bought silver, and paid an impoverished child to polish it. Their children—two sons, John and Robert—attended

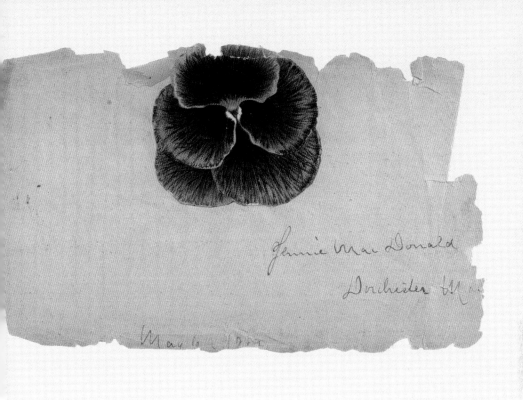

Milton Academy, then Bowdoin and Dartmouth, respectively, before passing their bar exams, and then assuming long if undistinguished careers in public service (patent office, planning commission). Their grandchildren mixed democratically in public schools, degrading their accents and expectations. Their great-grandchildren became the kind of people who wear sweatpants to restaurants.

I used to see some of these, sometimes, at Christmas parties— vague cousins of cousins who'd kept vaguely in touch. Our encounters lacked resonance of any kind, though perhaps I am a deaf man amid the loudest of bells. Anyhow, I no longer trifle with holidays. I see through their unblemished skins, their veils and suggestive hose, to the ghastly innards that roil beneath in steam and bile: all platitudes and placation and invitations to consume. Though as a motorist prone to nerves I appreciate the fluid intersections and ease of parking attributable to a holiday's absent traffic. We are confronted, aren't we, with difficult choices.

Colin A Chishom   Hyde Park Mass

Member well and bear in mind
a trusty friend is hard to find so
when you find him keep him fresh in
mine and dont jance[?] him for the
new
Annie McFalan

A low local boy—cowlicked, collars stained and wrinkled, importu-
nate in manner. Annie was kept away when possible.

Colin later worked as a millwright in Lowell, and performed as a
redoubtable batsman in the Merrimack Industrial League. Unmar-
ried, he rented a cottage at the rear of a widow's property on Lake
Street and drank two nights a week at the Scrimmage House, a workingman's saloon. He should have vanished into deserved oblivion had
he not been, in July of 1916, seen exposing his genitals to little girls
on the Market Street trolley. Detectives took from his rooms a car-
ton of inflammatory pamphlets distributed by the I.W.W., booklets of
pornographic line drawings, and a set of quite revolting picture postcards; they additionally discovered, buried in his tomato patch, the
communion shoe of Wee Ellie Connolly, a grocer's child who was, at
the time, six months missing. Ellie was later found living near Rochester with a brakeman of the New York Central—but no matter.

At the sensational trial, Benedict Chesterfield, an eminent anato-
mist summoned from the State Agricultural College at Amherst, tes-
tified that Colin's skull was characterized by structural aberrations—
see its convex *squama temporalis*, its emphatic amative locus—that
positioned it, on a spectrum of wholesomeness, nearer to the skull

of a Sumatran gibbon than to that of a conventional human. Apes are the most depraved and unbecoming of the greater beasts and lack the moral acumen and sexual control required for advanced society. Professor Chesterfield provided excellent plaster casts for the jury to handle.

During his incarceration Colin's literary taste and comprehension were discovered to be at a primary school level; his favorite book was *The Tale of Clarence Cowbell; or, The Twice-Eaten Pie*, and he nightly traced the hornlike pad of his index finger across its raised oversized type. His favorite song was "The Spaniard That Blighted My Life," which he sang, in a surprising countertenor, at his guards' slightest prompting. He was electrocuted in the Charles Street Jail, March 1917, before a whooping gallery, following a final performance of the above.

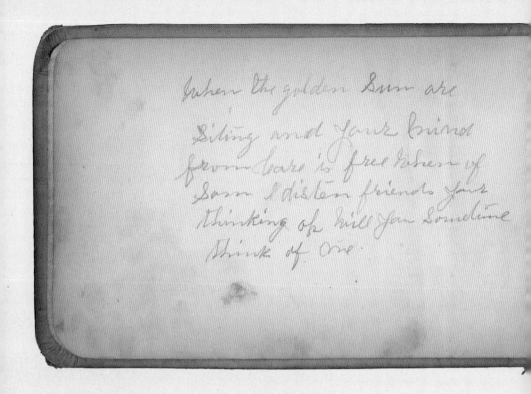

The writer of these lines, which continue on 5v, fails to identify herself as more than "Mary." This was a not unwise choice, given the confused, insupportable nature of this little imitation of verse she has recorded. So obviously "she": the angles of the lettering, the even lines, the even spacing. Ordered thought is, was, of great importance to young women; the trait accompanies their superior hygiene. Anyway, it's almost endearing. The dear tries so hard to impress us, and falls so comically short in the fundamentals. One hundred years later, in our age as soaked in irony as a holiday cake in rum, someone might produce this on purpose and be praised for his droll genius. Our age may also be soaked in sincerity—I'm not sure what our favorite vloggers have most lately declaimed—but sincerity would work just as well, if we accept authorial naïveté.

I have worked a bit at poetry myself. The following, for instance, I produced on a balcony at Long Bay, Antigua, during my second honeymoon with my first wife, Naomi G., an "artist" who now spends her days painting murals of dolphins and conches and frolicking surfers in her cozy Laguna Beach cottage, the mortgage of which I am compelled to subsidize per the terms of our divorce settlement.

[4v]

When the golden sun are
siting and your mind
from care is free when of
some disten friends your
thinking of will you sometime
think of me

My camera's paroxysm caught today
The gruesome girls at worship,
Prone before the violet ribbing of the sea.
Brilliantly bare, glassily impassive:
How fiery it felt,
Their comprehensive, cradling temptation—
Like tidings of my own extinction.
Later, toppled by the drinks I'd had,
Their toppling storm,
I watched a drunk and poignant dawn.

This is, of course, quite good—but I wouldn't dare think good enough. Just because one can versify, I'm saying, does not mean that one should. The nineteenth century might better have remembered this. So might have the twentieth. I might better remember this. In the winters of our spirits we ought to lock ourselves indoors, and peer as silent as monks through our leaded windows onto the furious snow.

Love is like a scotch snuff
you will take a pinch
And that's enough

Miss Annie McFare[?]

What a fun girl, what a laugh and a good time, Annie must have been. "Scotch snuff" is, apparently, a powder-fine preparation of conventional tobacco snuff. An unladylike habit to cultivate, I suppose. One can imagine much moral terror being attached to it. A pinch, the merest pinch, and a girl will be drinking beer and wearing French hose, raising the hem of her skirt in a disgusting wharfside saloon, to the delight of Italian and Portuguese stevedores with oiled mustaches and careless sideburns. Note, too, the guarded attitude toward love, which leads as inevitably to spread legs and ruined wombs as the abuse of exotic substances. Annie, I'm told, after decades of abstinence, became an incessant smoker in her elder years—soft packs of Pall Malls, most often wrinkled or bent, pulled from the bottom of her cavernous, floral-patterned knit purse. Her closed-up sitting room, as she sat and read *Paris Match*, or listened to a Red Sox game on the wireless, resembled, with its trapped smoke, an ill-lit foundry, or a sulfur spring in a closed cavern, and inspired many hushed coughs on the part of my careful, silent father. She dropped ash everywhere and relieved her dry, acrid mouth with butterscotch candies. How delightfully her house must have whiffed on a summer's evening after a ball game, as her girl in the yellow kitchen baked scrod and boiled cab-

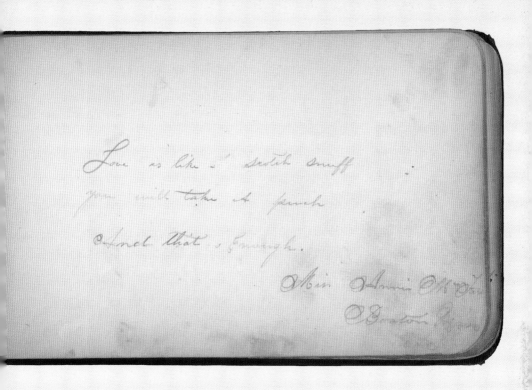

bage, and Annie uncorked a bottle of crude sherry, and the heat went unrelieved.

I used to enjoy an occasional cigarette myself, but the habit loses its elegance as one ages. One must be young and gaunt, I think, and inclined to dress in dark colors. Someone fat and dove-gray, huddled in a service entrance, taking his brief, compromised puffs, is a figure of pure tragedy. Later on he eats fast food hamburgers, four to an order, wolfing them at a sticky plastic table, beneath the filthy restaurant's bleak fluorescence, with guilt-spurred alacrity. I have concerns about the character of a man who cultivates so visible an oral fixation.

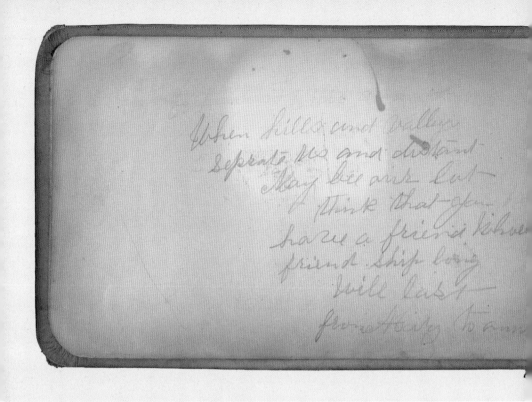

There are entirely too many girls called Mary born in this era, into this milieu. There are entirely too many girls called Mary who appear in this autograph book. The handwriting appears, to my dilettante's eye, unique, as does the loose command of language. I expect this Mary was a child, almost but not quite precocious—or perhaps some damaged, tolerated neighborhood figure who'd been kicked in the head while cleaning a horse's hoof, or had her skull pinched while exiting Mummy's narrow birth canal. Yes—I prefer the latter, I think. A block-shouldered, cone-crowned maiden, with haphazard hair and high uneven bangs, always stealing sugar cubes, always finding orphaned squirrels, never more than a spare part in the games of the neighborhood children. We should be sympathetic. Mary meant so well, and tried so hard; or so I assume. At least she was literate.

Here's a further scrap of dashed-off verse, just to demonstrate how easy it is. One cannot and should not attempt to pin the origin of inspiration. But I suppose the upstart drama shown last night on TV news—the rioting and combat of equally unkempt, equally humorless, equally delinquent bands of adolescent toughs, in some squalid urban American setting, in a state no one has visited, and then a parallel event in a foreign locale, a beige desert place (mud bricks and min-

When hills and valleys
Seprate us and distant
May bee our lot
think that you
have a friend whoes
friend ship long
will last
from Mary to annie

arets) the name of which I failed to catch—cast intriguing shadows across the ridges of my brain.

> There, untrammeled,
> Our emphasis remains.
> From sorrows that linger,
> Different evocations are returned.
> Perhaps aristocrats,
> Holding historical sentiments,
> Developed satire:
> The aristocratic clique,
> Longing for exile.

I don't watch television, by the way. I don't even own a television. But the hotel room in which I presently work does have one mounted on the wall, and its chatter and colorful flicker provide a measure of comfort at night, and an illusion of company, which I now and again find agreeable. More bothersome is the laminate veneer of the night-stand, which reflects a garish white light when the lamp is switched on. The bar downstairs, which is made of salvaged driftwood and decorated with nets—I'm very close to the sea—is charming.

[6r]

To Annie

In life's golden chain
Let one link bear the name
of Agnes

Cousin Agnes Carmichael, a year Annie's senior, was a frequent guest at birthday parties, holiday suppers, Sunday teas, et cetera. My handful of photographs—or, I should say, a handful of photographs briefly in my possession—reveal a shockingly tall, shockingly broad figure; her bones should have been hollow for her to successfully locomote. Two angular teeth project over her lip, with an obtuse triangle of shade between them. A shaggy brow on whose prominence one could crack walnuts obscures the pits in which her protrusive all-white eyes are mounted. A sweep through the sea by her mighty hands could propel galleys. I would expect her to steal infants from their cradles and carry them away to witch caves, trading them for handfuls of sweetmeats and shiny trinkets, or to menace many a wandering salesman and tramp as she emerges from a barn in torn, unclasped overalls, bellowing, frothing, hay in hair, pitchfork raised like a javelin.

But Agnes was sound. She attended Miss Porter's School, then Wellesley, in both spots acquiring, with her liberal arts, all sorts of *ideas*, as sometimes happened. Over the subsequent decades, living in the carriage house of her parents', and subsequently brother's, Newton property, she campaigned for suffrage, temperance, and social relief. Though her enthusiasm was appreciated, it was preferred that

To Annie—

In life's golden chain
Let one link bear the name
of Agnes.

Agnes confine her efforts to pamphleteering and letters to editors; this was much less distracting, and she did possess a fine, if hectoring and intrusive, natural style. She also tried her hand at magazine fiction, and published, in serial form, a novel called *Murder in the Blue Boudoir*, as Arnold Carmichael. A millionaire's wife is found dead, bludgeoned, in a drawing room locked from the inside; only a prim but good-humored visiting spinster can unravel the mystery, a dense farrago of mistaken identities, cross-dressing servants, secret telegrams, artificial limbs, peepholes, and poisoned treacle cake. The magazine in which it appeared, *Dark Cloak Adventure All-Story*, declared bankruptcy before remitting payment, alas.

Agnes never married, never had children, but did raise, in her subdued eld, a champion line of Maine coons, the descendants of which still receive ribbons and little cat-shaped trophies in piss-reeking auditoriums across the continent.

Dear Annie:—

When far away my love your care

And to some little fellow marri

Remember me for old time's sake

And send me a piece of wedding c

Yours as ever,

Clarence C. Mudie

Boston, Mass.   #85   Chicago, Ill.

Clarence Mudie passed biannually through New England on fundraising missions for the Pan-American Apostolic Legion. He was an elongated figure with a high forehead and greased, flopping hair, whose cornflower eyes were ever ashine with either Christly passion or the glaze of the bottle, depending on the hour. While in Boston he stayed at the Hyde Park home of his sister, Isabelle Mudie Rhodes, whose daughter Dottie appears on a subsequent page of this volume. The local children, Annie very much included, loved to gather about him to hear of his exotic adventures. In New York City he ate in the same restaurant as the Barrymores, and recommended the beefsteak. In Washington he met an Ethiopian prince—an immense tawny Negro draped in silks as fine as any bishop's. In Minnesota he saw buffalo and painted tepees and said "howgh" to an Indian sachem who wore buckskins and full feathers. It was all so *of the world*; one hated to return to the crushing familiarity of one's everyday soda counters and milkmen and canopies of elm.

Number 85 of *Marian Youth Weekly* contains two pieces by Mudie. "A Night at the Circus" is a short story recounting an adolescent boy's experience at an unsavory traveling show. The lights and music are garish, as are the midway spectacles, and odors of cigar smoke

[6v]

Dear Annie:—
When far away my love your carried,
And to some little fellow married,
Remember me for old time's sake,
And send me a piece of wedding cake.
Yours as ever,
Clarence E. Mudie
Chicago Ills.

Boston, Mass.
July 6, 1896.

#85   "A Night at the Circus."   "Chutes"

and whiskey prevail throughout the tattered tents; ill-shaven, foul-mouthed clowns threaten the boy when he interrupts their card game; Doughty Doris, the World's Strongest Woman, puts aside her barbells and tries to lure the boy into the back of her wagon; and a wrong turn leads into Leon the Lion's enclosure, where, as the boy prays for salvation if not safety, furious Leon—a scarred, snarling man-eater—lies down before him and gently grooms his paws; the boy runs home, where his loving parents await and embrace him, and provide him with milk and tea cake. "Chutes" is a bit of doggerel that lists and describes dozens of opportunities for young people to slide into hellfire. Premarital kissing, petty theft, sips of papa's liquor, elopement, foul language, skipped confession, failure to observe proper hygiene—that sort of thing.

Enjoy your pleasure as it lasts: cling to and savor it:
For you shall know no more its like, once fallen to the pit!

The ground quite literally opens up under all these naughty boys and girls.

To Annie

May your cross be strewn with flowers.

Is the sincere wish of
S.C.[?]W.

"May your path be strewn with flowers" is the commonplace expression, as you're likely aware, reader. The simplest sentiments proliferate. "May your cross be strewn with flowers" is, I believe, a unique variation—my research has not turned up its like: a little play on words. I would like to think that a morbid joke was intended, suggesting a floral arrangement displayed at a funeral, but I doubt it. Girls of that era, of that age, of Annie's particular circle, scarcely had humor at all; and death loomed over them to a degree we can't fathom—on the splattered pillowcases of tuberculosis wards, in the fever-soaked, twisted bedsheets of quarantined bedrooms, silent in the bloody hands of midwives. Perhaps the writer wished for Annie an attractive centerpiece at Easter supper, or something dull like that.

Meanwhile—SCW? SLW? SBW? I don't know who this might be. One of Annie's school chums, or another young acquaintance, I expect. Annie had a propensity for sociability that was not heritable, and even in her that propensity failed to carry past middle age. Elder, widowed Annie stalked all day about her silent house in a state of abject terror—that a clock might chime, a phone might ring, a noisy truck might pass outside. She glared every noontime through the peephole at her mailman, unable to take full breaths, patting her throat, mak-

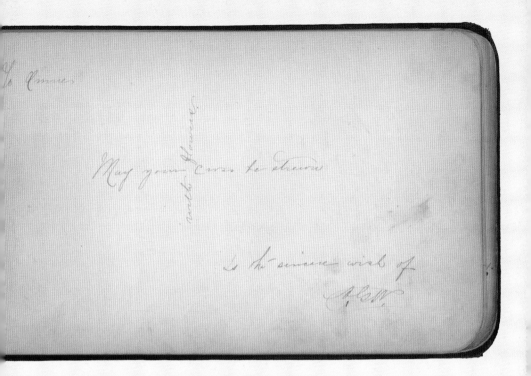

ing soft chattering sounds like an aroused cat, his service somehow a violation, staring dumbfounded when a stack of white envelopes fell through the mail slot and brushed the quilted toes of her slippers.

I find I'm aging into a similar state myself. I become a stammering moron when addressing waiters and shop clerks, and am loath to make of them demands or peculiar requests. I can only speak on the telephone if I deploy a false voice, a smoothed and jovial too-loud voice that terrifies the other party. I prefer to stand on a train than to take an empty seat beside a stranger. I must have my hair cut once per week—otherwise I hear whispers, laughs. I see on the map how the road I drive climbs and curves.

Friend Nan.

Though oceans wide between
us roll,
And distant be our lot
Though we may never meet again
My friend "forget me not"

Yours Tru
& Don

At summer's end Charlotte "Lottie" Douglas left Boston on RMS *Exaltation*, of the White Star Line, aboard which she shared a modest suite with her spinster aunt Betty Douglas, and Betty's lifelong maid. Returned to her family's country house (Churchbell End, in Buckinghamshire), she renewed her private studies, which consisted of homemaker's arithmetic, charcoal drawing, a little Latin, and lots of gazing out at the rain, half wistful, half in pursuit of embedded patterns that implied existential meaning. And much riding, her favorite pastime: she was a skilled jumper and could run down a fox more ably than most sporting gentlemen. As autumn passed Lottie developed a rapport with the new groom, Tom Lynch, a square-jawed Black Irish fellow who had been, it was said, imprisoned at Kilmainham, but who possessed a soft, dreamy, winning demeanor and a stunning way with horse and hound alike. They fell in love: such occurs. She was fifteen, he twenty-three, but this was the way of things then, more or less; perhaps less. Anyhow, discreet trysts were enjoyed—in haylofts, in horse stalls, in the shuttered guest wing, in copses of alder, in the reeds along the River Stoke—and fevered, nauseous, not to say nauseating, words were whispered. In spring they ran off together, and spent four months in a Roscommon croft, Tom tending the creatures

[7v]

Friend now.

Though oceans wide between
us roll,
And distant be our lot
Though we may never meet again
My friend "forget me not"

Yours Truly,
L. Douglas

of a nearby estate, Lottie at home gamely stirring stewpots and sweeping the hearth, their evenings together in the long northern half-light sensually spent—until one misty August afternoon, when a coughing motorcar sprang up the track from town and discharged Lottie's father and twin elder brothers. They kicked the door from its rusted hinges, and when Tom, who had been pouring whiskey from a ceramic jug as he sat at the kitchen table, awaiting his tin plate of beans in gravy, stood, Papa Douglas shot him with his service revolver (as he had, years earlier, many a Zulu, many a Pashtun). Lottie changed from her modest wools and linens into the silk dress, sable coat, and bonnet that her father sulkily provided. Her brothers buried Tom in the garden, covering the disturbed earth with fieldstones. In time Lottie married Sir Albert Culpepper, the well-known barrister and Liberal MP, lived in his fine Highgate home, bore his children and wore his furs, and died in a bed that would have cost as much as a luxury sedan, had it not been the legacy of some seventeenth-century ancestral lordling. She sent Annie a hand-painted Christmas card every year, always with a fabulous royal stamp.

Dear Annie,

Within this page so pure and white
Let none but friends presume to write
And may each word with friendship given
Direct the readers thoughts to Heaven.

Sincerely Your Friend,
Minnie Campbell
Vanceboro
Maine.

June 8, 1888

Andrew McFarlane kept a fishing camp on Spednic Lake, a wild place on the New Brunswick border. Each July he tied up his business, packed a trunk, and boarded a northbound B&M (the Micmac Flyer, generally) at North Station to spend three unfettered weeks in the woods, gutting trout, drinking applejack, and reading lurid gentlemen's magazines in the pale, unceasing twilight. In time his wife convinced him to include his family at least peripherally on these adventures; a lodge was put up at Vanceboro, and the McFarlanes gained a second home, which they never tired of mentioning. Blueberry pies cooling on sills, emitting cartoon curtains of sweet steam. Bodies sprawled on porch swings, adoze between languid flicks of fly swatters and Chinese fans. Swims in a frankly quite filthy-looking pond; dangling from the end of a launch, in the present day, I trailed my fingers through its coffee-colored water, and came away with grounds beneath my nails. Such idylls come to nothing, mean nothing, of course. I spent my childhood summers watching television and engaging in self-abuse, and yet have landed, I think, well ahead of any McFarlane, in finer comfort. It just shows you that nothing shows you anything. Present-day accommodation in Vanceboro remains "rustic," by the way; I fled my lodgings

Dear Annie

Within this page so pure and white
Let none but friends presume to write
And may each word with friendship given
Direct the readers Thoughts to Heaven.

Sincerely Your Friend
Minnie Campbell
Vanceboro
Maine.

June 8th 1888

at four a.m., driving south at high speed, clawing at my inner thighs, stopping in Bangor to buy and apply permethrin.

Meanwhile, I fear I have little to report on Minnie Campbell. It's not an uncommon surname, is it, and many county records were destroyed by a fire in the 1930s; and it was not my preference to tarry in remotest Maine, where one is never certain whether being eaten by bears or impaled on a stray syringe is the paramount threat. Let's assume she was narrow of frame, possessed limp drab hair that she pasted to her too-tall skull, wore her silver crucifix always on the outside of her clothes, read only uplifting literature, obsessed over the moral failings of her (scarce) neighbors, never married, kept terriers, and died in sweaty terror at her unabsolved sins.

I am as annoyed as you, reader, by Minnie's attempt to rhyme "given" with "heaven." What accent would lead a person to this, I don't know, but hers must have been dreadful.

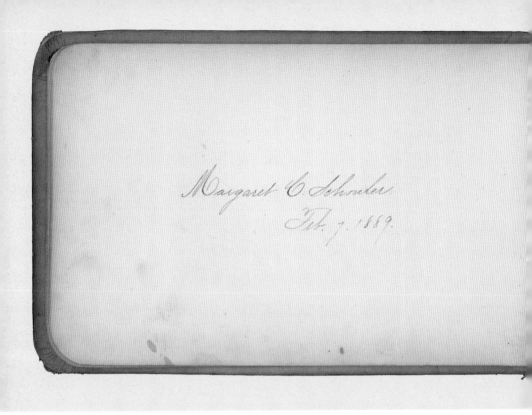

A dark, skinny girl with a body like a palisade stake, and a face like that stake's sharpened tip. Her eyes were forever obscure behind spectacle lenses as thick as a diving helmet's window. Though often taken for a Jew due to her surname, Margaret was, in fact, of an old, genteel Scottish line, bulging with lawmakers, scholars, and eminent soldiers, and could claim distant but traceable kinship with the third Viscount Glenwhilly, albeit through bastardry. She thought of Annie as irremediably middle class—I'd like to think she thought so, anyhow. I would have thought so. Her autograph uplifts this album, I think she thought.

Despite her narrow figure and prim demeanor, Margaret was, for two consecutive years, the champion eater of ice cream at the annual Pickard School Summer's Day Festival. On the second occasion she ate fourteen scoops of vanilla in one turn of the dean's egg timer. Somehow, this roused in her history master, a mutton-chopped widower called Peter Trumbull, a furious ardor. We all have our quirks: I'm keen on eyebrows, for instance, and believe that they should be as black and powerful as a gorilla's flexed bicep. Peter maintained a perfect propriety for the rest of Margaret's academic career, save, I imagine, for yearning looks and cold sponges pressed to fevered bald pates, but upon her graduation he came banging the knocker—a vast brass face of Janus—at the many-gabled Schouler manse, carrying with him a bottle of 1881 Clos Vougeot and a typed copy of his curriculum vitae. A relevant figure of the household was convinced, and Margaret wed Peter that autumn. Annie attended both the ceremony and the reception, and presented them with a porcelain sugar dish, later regifted to a housekeeper.

Margaret and Peter are an amusing couple in their wedding portrait. He looks like her grandfather. She looks like his walking stick. I'm not surprised no children were conceived. There are physical limitations, you know, even within compatible species. Peter died in 1903, and Margaret lived on in his stale Back Bay flat, alone save for occasional intervals with shih tzus, amid his overflowing bookshelves and musty couches, for all her remaining days, of which there were some sixteen thousand.

[9r]

To Annie

Kindest wishes of

Mrs. D. B. McDonald

Daniel Bryce McDonald, of Brookline, was a vigorous delight. Scarcely five feet in height, orphaned and ill in his impoverished childhood, rough-voiced (pinched sinus, liquid throat), lowly accented, prone to unflattering weight gain, unpleasant to look at (an odd hairline, a bulbous pitted nose), he surmounted his inborn deficiencies through sheer energy and bluster. At eighteen, using the meager bequest handed off by his grandmother, Daniel purchased a rail pass and went west, fortune-seeking. He harvested wheat for a season outside of Omaha. He tended bar at a Fort Collins saloon. He fought the Shoshone in Idaho, killing three men and taking as souvenirs a bear claw necklace and a handful of molars that he kept in an ivory dice box. He caught the largest trout then on record while fishing in the North Umpqua River in Oregon; a commemorative plaque remains in the archives of the Douglas County Historical Club at Sutherlin, though I was unable to view it personally. He panned for gold at Bodie, California, and made enough from that to buy a stake in a prospective silver mine near Reno. He made enough from *that* to travel back to Boston in a private sleeping car, lease a townhouse near the Public Garden, fill his wardrobe with fine suits, and buy his way into a respectable business—linens, as it happened. He joined the same Episcopal con-

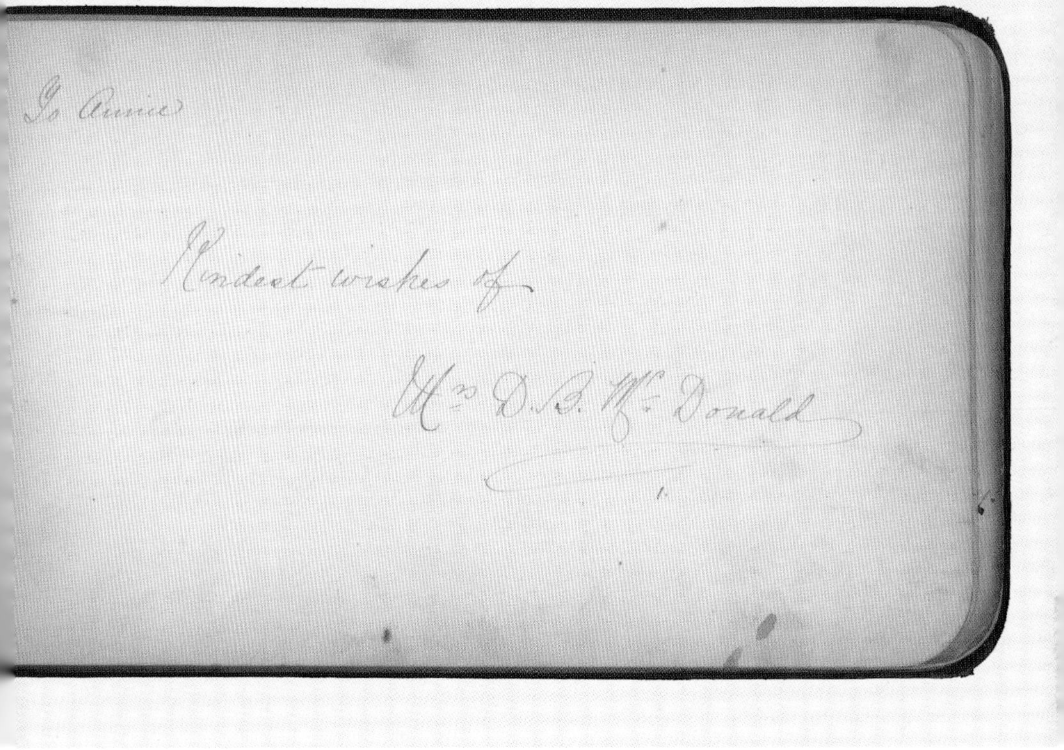

To Annie

Kindest wishes of

Mrs D.B. McDonald

gregation of which the Provost of Harvard and Senator Hoar were members. He married and fathered three sons, whom he raised with rationed affection and in Spartan comfort, in the name of discipline and strength and an ordered self. He donated great sums to the fire brigade, which named an engine after him. He ate roast beef with politicians, and his whispered councils were the subject of speculation by newspaper columnists.

Andrew McFarlane found Daniel amusing company. There was always an anecdote, and he possessed a surprising capacity for reflection, and for wine. Daniel's wife, Martha, who signed this album, had kind eyes and a heavy bust, and wore elaborate lace shawls that she knitted all by herself.

To Annie

If ever a husband you will have
And he these lines may read
Tell him of your youthful days
And kiss him once for me W. D. Chisholm
Vanceboro NB

June 10th 1888

Of no relation to Colin, whom you remember from an earlier page, W. D. Chisholm—Wanda Doherty—was the daughter of a family friend. These Chisholms visited often at Vanceboro to take the country air, much to the discomfort of the McFarlanes, who were forced for entire weeks by such company to dress for supper, and to mute their habitual bickering. Wanda died in childbirth; her son survived and went on to do nothing worth noting.

Annie, of course, did marry—Charles Phelps Dawes, a decent if unexciting chap, in 1899. The son of Abraham Dawes of Salem, a ship's captain in the Orient trade, and Mehitable Phelps, young Charles was gentle and studious, a lover of Romantic poetry and taxidermied birds. He had become a physician, to his father's disappointment—Abraham had hoped that Charles, if not going to sea, might take up law with an eye toward the legislature. These were days, remember, in which medicine remained a craft, just barely glorified, and chockablock with nonsense compared to those of the glazier and the stonemason. I suppose there's something to be said for healing and helping—it's useful to have healers and helpers about—though such urges are foreign to me. It's hard enough to heal, or to help, oneself. From my vantage it would have been better for Charles to have gone

[9v]

To Annie

If ever a husband you will have
And he these lines may read
Tell him of your youthful days
And kiss him once for me

W. D. Chisholm
Vanceboro, Me

June 10th 1888

into oil or munitions, or to have invented radio, or to have defrauded widows, whatever, than to have been a martyr to the care of unknown strangers. I'd prefer any circumstance that would have left me with a livable annuity.

Annie would have liked this as well. Charles's gracious accent and imperial whiskers suggested a finer future than he would or temperamentally could provide, to her perpetual disappointment. Still, he was handsome and tidy, well-read, good with children, and tolerant of Andrew McFarlane's Electral competitiveness, participating at family gatherings in countless swimming, sprinting, lifting, and drinking contests of which Annie was ever the judge. He died in 1936, while returning from a house call in the dawn hours, when his Packard was run off the parkway and into the Mystic River by a bread truck whose driver had fallen asleep.

[10r]

To Annie;—

May your voyage through life,
Be as happy, and free,
As the dancing wave,
On the deep, blue sea.

Your sincere friend,
May Horton

Boston, Jan. 10th '89.

May Horton, a delphinid calf of a girl, dreamed always of the sea. Indeed, she talked so incessantly of the sea—statistics of volume and depth; its curious inhabitants; the aerodynamics of sails; the gorgeous, useful stars above it—that many of her grinning contemporaries wished she would fill her pockets with stones and walk out into it. May loved to sit on the breakwater at Pleasure Bay and hear the waves, and to swim at Carson Beach, until an outbreak of polio caused her mother to forbid public bathing. She read nautical tales, admiring in particular the likes of *Fanny Campbell*, *Fierce Island*, and *Admiral Sadie Bedford*. Her school essays, when topics were freely chosen, were on Oliver Perry, Admiral Nelson, the Leeward Islands, the Labrador Current, the trireme, the astrolabe, Sir Francis Drake. Hurricane season— its black clouds sprinting above shorelines, its vengeful maritime spirit punishing the impious land—filled her with brutish delight, like a crusader sniffing the smoke and blood in some razed Saracen town. She carried a compass on a watch chain and went on hardtack fasts and employed a sextant as a paperweight. She thrilled at a stroll along the harbor front (escorted, of course) and gleaned strange meaning from the glyphic mess made by its masts and rigging and erupting

To Annie; —

May your voyage through life,
Be as happy and free,
As the dancing waves,
On the deep, blue sea.
Your sincere friend
May Horton

...rton, Jan. 10th '99.

stacks. Every ferry she rode felt as if it must bound for the shores of Elysium, though Nantasket and Provincetown had to suffice.

In 1893 May married John Hayward, a lieutenant in the army, and made house in Topeka, his hometown. Lt. Hayward died of yellow fever in Cuba during our imperial jaunt of 1898. May remained in Topeka, raising their son, John Jr., who I think owned a hardware store, or a hobby shop—something of that nature. The most substantial body of water she ever again visited in person was Big Spirit Lake, Iowa, where she spent one Fourth of July week at her daughter-in-law's parents' cottage. It rained every day, and all smelled of algae and gasoline.

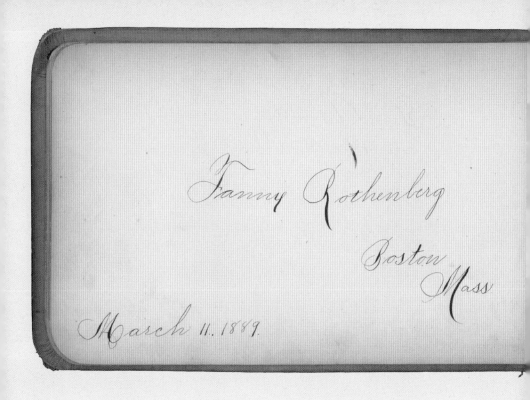

The Rothenberg family owned Rothenberg's, a department store on Summer Street downtown known for its elegant displays and the dignified modesty of its advertisements; Fanny attended the Pickard School with Annie, and came over for several casual suppers and holiday celebrations. Fanny wasn't Jewish, but rather the descendant of a Hessian deserter, much to the disappointment of Annie's mother, who harbored fantasies of converting Fanny, and being thereby awarded by the parish priest several hundreds of papal points, redeemable for gaudy silks, gold cruciform baubles, reduced tenures in purgatory, and the like. Fanny married a flash boy from New York, moved to the Upper East Side, and ceased to communicate with any of her old friends, for which I can scarcely blame her. I think her granddaughter, an Emeline Sorrell, created the Environmental Sexuality program at Bard, but I have performed, I admit, only the most perfunctory research.

Rothenberg's was liquidated during the very first decade in which the relevance of department stores was eclipsed by that of shopping malls, and those prescient surviving members of the Rothenberg dynasty ran to Arizona, speculating effectively there on real estate, furnishing subsequent generations with private incomes and inherited membership privileges at golf courses throughout the Valley of

[10v]

Fanny Rothenberg

Boston
Mass

March 11, 1889.

the Sun. The store's space has since been occupied by, among other more or less unsuccessful enterprises, a fondue restaurant (Le Joli Pot; I was taken once to a birthday party at their Burlington location, and suffered afterward my first pancreatic attack) and a reseller of consumer electronics (its owner ran for lieutenant governor on a platform of technocracy and muted racism, and was later prosecuted for tax avoidance). Presently the building is empty, and is to be refurbished and reconfigured for luxury condominiums (luxurious, anyway, to the extent that any accommodation in Boston could be deemed luxurious), pending final approval by the Redevelopment Authority. The Neoclassical cornices and red bricks of its facade are to be preserved as treasures of history, though they look no different from anything else on their block, or any other block. The condos, in the developer's prospectus, seem nice enough: reclaimed tigerwood plank flooring, chef's kitchens with Wolf appliances, bathroom surfaces of purest marble, a roof deck and swimming pool and spa, a gymnasium with on-demand personal trainers. If you're the sort of person content to be entombed in a condo. I dream of tasteful drawing rooms that overlook green fields and deer parks. So does everyone I know, or wish to know.

David Bowles
Malden Mass

We'll assume that the David Bowles I've discovered is the same David Bowles whose signature appears in this book. The path of discovery is arduous: a steep and dusty grade lined with brier patches and poison oak, interrupted by fallen logs and swollen creeks, menaced by coyotes and catamounts—particularly when one seeks to discover the insignificant.

In pursuit of David I visited the wet, fragrant basement of a Malden triple-decker, pawing its mess of hoarded artifacts, ruining my white shirt and my fingernails. The place was owned by an Elaine Flannery, some Bowles niece or close cousin, whose unworldly deafness infuriated me through the half-dozen phone calls it took to clarify my purpose. I thought a homicide perhaps in order when I was at last invited over: a mercy killing. But Elaine proved a cordial old sparrow, and I drank her rancid coffee, and tolerated her senile chirps. My rented Audi went somehow unmolested in the street.

David was a round-faced, big-necked boy with thin, unruly hair, and in possession of at least one passable suit, declares the photocopy of a photograph paper-clipped to the folder before me. I assume his cheeks would have been as red as a smoke-choked sunset—as though viewed, given his perpetual sheen of sweat, through a pane

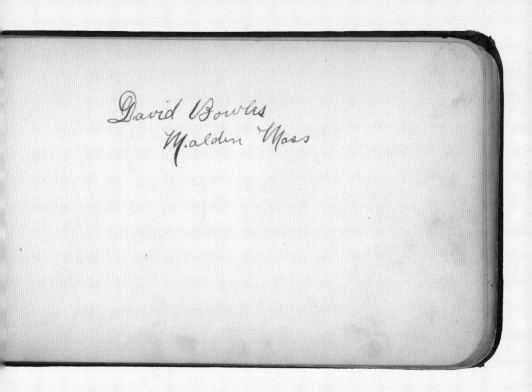

David Bowles
Malden Mass

of filthy glass. An attorney and alderman's son, he attended Harvard and earned a useful diploma in the classics. A dinner party was held in June 1894 to celebrate both his twenty-first birthday and his graduation. Alas, just before the cheese course, he fell dramatically ill, much to the unease of Mrs. Everett Stevens, the mayor's wife, who detected a sexual menace in David's low moans and cradled abdomen. He died writhing overnight in his childhood bed, having consumed, like King Henry, a surfeit of eels and claret. The eels were served *à l'Anglaise*, stewed in port and butter; the claret, though mediocre, was at least presented in a pretty decanter of Baccarat crystal. Based on his mother's later correspondence, preserved in one of Elaine's many moth-and-mouse-chewed boxes, I assume David died of peritonitis. Indulgence deprives us once more of essential insights into Attic grammar and prosody.

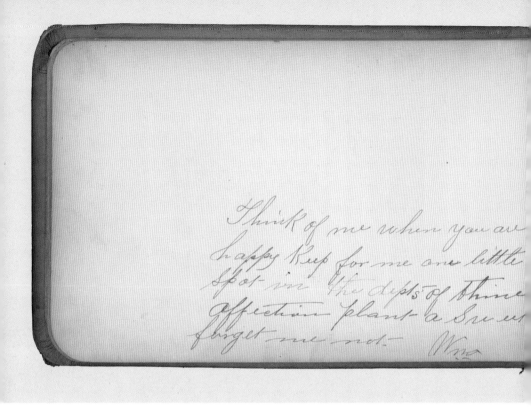

William Cutler, a ginger boy whose father owned a millinery on River Street, lived diagonally across the street from the McFarlanes, in a white farmhouse with an excellent rose garden; he raked the leaves of his neighbors' lawns and brought them buckets of apples from the twin trees in his own backyard, never expecting payment, monetary or in kind, and always tidied the leavings of the Cutler family retriever, Endymion, either with a coal shovel or his own handkerchief, as circumstances dictated; he joined, in time, the priesthood, eventually becoming the Vicar General of Schenectady.

William McBride was a maternal second cousin, a resident of Framingham, who came now and again to supper when his business—silverware—took him to Boston; fond of bean plates, unable to grow a full mustache, missing a front tooth from a schoolyard scrap, crimson nose, purple knuckles.

William "Billy" Cote was the son of Jack Cote, Andrew McFarlane's lead salesman; a flippant, foul-mouthed boy given to petty theft and surreptitious drinking, but charming, and an energetic and creative prankster; he became a police captain in southern New Hampshire, in a decomposing mill town, zestfully enforcing any unwritten sundown law he could imagine.

[11v]

Think of me when you are
happy keep for me one little
spot in the depts of thine
affections plant a sweet
forget me not.

Wm[?]

William David Sheffield, the son of the McFarlane family's phy-sician, expressed a passing romantic interest in Annie, never acted upon, likely illusory, but always mentioned by her as a lusher field left ungrazed when she discussed her husband's shortcomings, and the shortcomings of their son. Sheffield made lots of money in insurance, built Sheffield House, a Tudor Revival pile, in West Hartford (tours Tuesdays through Sundays), married an earl's daughter, and, upon his young retirement, wrote aesthetically dubious but publishable, read-able romantic novels after the manner of Sir Walter Scott.

We know, then, a handful of possible Williams. We can scarcely contain our delight at this abundance. We can scarcely contain our disdain for the "thine" in the note, an archaism even in 1889, a ver-itable flint axe belonging in the toolkit of a precious, skins-wearing, protohuman hack. We detest William.

[12r]

Forget me not forget me never
Or until yonder sun shall set forever

F.[?]

This intimate habit—the recording of a mere initial—makes research difficult. Intimacy is two parts dependence, one part arrogance, and a dash of the limp wrist, all poured into the cavity where the glands of selfhood would glisten and throb, had they not been withered by onslaughts of self-abuse and poor nutrition. I would like to experience a world in which we've ceased to pretend to know others—or at least one in which others ceased to pretend to know me: this would suffice—and our exchanges could be restrained and kept to topics such as the day's degree of sunlight and the decency of our wine. Nicknames should be abolished, too, while we're at this. They diminish the named and imbue the namer with undue power. Those same namers like to touch your elbow when they shake your hand, and to repeat the name they've imposed with needless frequency over the course of your ghastly conversation. Their teeth are often very white.

Anyhow, F. appears content to be forgotten once the sun dies, an event that science says will not occur for another five billion years. But it's happened sooner, poor F., it's happened already. F. is a flicker in Annie's fading shade, which has itself ceased to exist as any more than a projection of yours truly. Sometimes, as I examine a family photograph, her painted eyebrows thicken and arch, and burst like spring

daffodils into the angular profusion of my own. This happens, too, to lips—her chewed, downturned putties transform into my beard-decked duck's bill. I don't mean to diminish my efforts in this volume, mind—to write history is to wrap oneself in it, pinning and shearing as you form its fabric about your body. All the great historians have struggled to reconcile this with their pretensions of objectivity, I'm sure. Overweight men in windowless basement offices moaning and rubbing their bald, glistening temples, indigo archipelagoes of sweat staining their cheap button-downs, all hunched over desks cluttered with paper cups, burrito foils, and deadly boring sources. No tenure. No lovers. Leased studios, all filthy. Vacations in tents. I bear no such burdens. A layman's approach liberates, even if it wins neither allies nor accolades, and victories are victories.

Why this deletion? Appalling penmanship? One prefers a pretty book, but there are lots of ugly examples, hither and tither, on other pages. Barroom language? Annie did blush, even in late life, at the word "bottom," even in reference to pickle barrels and riverbeds. She once slapped my father, and took back his birthday gift, a Streamliner model kit, as punishment for impiety, after bad Dad cried "jeez!" in response to a startling thunderclap. Unchristian thought? Obviously such mattered to Annie, or at least their potential appearance. (We must suppose that Christian concerns are limited to matters of decorum and sexual restraint.) Nevertheless, I've found evidence of contraband volumes passed between giggling, protoironic girls at the Pickard and Vanceboro Schools: *Lazenby's Concupiscent Tales*, *The Birchinghide Papers*, *Rendezvous at Chateau Frottage*. The contrast between this giggling, titillated young Annie, and the older Annie of her marital and postmarital beds—those sarcophagi, flanked by grotesque demon statues, etched with hieroglyphs warning of dire curses, all layered in dust two inches thick—amuses. Unacceptable politics? Any politics at all would blemish what's meant to be a wee girl's dewy record. Still. As with everything else in her life, Annie tolerated a limited range of opinions, centered on her own unsupported if not insupportable

[12v]

[effaced]

positions. Against hick-y, hysterical, pink-bellied Bryan—how quickly comes metropolitan snobbery to upstart Scotch-Irish—and in favor of uplifting southerly browns by expropriating their haphazard small-holdings for civilized, agronomist-certified plantations dispatching discounted tropical fruits across the globe. Annie liked to add a mashed banana to her ice milk, for the potassium. Against the second Roosevelt, who rushed society like a naked Indian, his dangling dick in a blood-red sheath, cracking the foundations of order with his savage hammer, decapitating pioneers with his sickle. She liked Taft (several Tafts) and, in later years, the John Birch Society, whose literature she displayed on her coffee table, and she chaired a Ladies' Committee to restore redlining in her affluent suburb of residence. There's no way that I might tell, short of employing a forensicist, which is not at all in keeping with the spirit of my approach.

[13r]

Miss Annie McFarlin[?]

Think of me long
Think of me Ever
Think of the Happy
Times we spent to
gether

Miss Maggie M
Donald
Boston

By 1922, Maggie lived in Cob Village, a maritime hamlet on Buzzards Bay. Nowadays it's a place where, in gray-shingled buildings decked in collages of netting and buoys, "artists" display lifeless watercolors on maritime themes to noisy weekenders. All the shops sell commemorative sweatshirts and gift boxes of stale saltwater taffy. A plate of fried wonderment, bathed in tartar sauce and malt vinegar, is the seaside's great consolation, but in Cob Village I could find only overpriced cafés overlooking the black timbers and gull shit of the rotting wharf. My twelve-dollar sandwich featured "microgreens" and tasted like a vacuum bag; my nine-dollar glass of pinot grigio was an oak-and-hairball formulation only a dissolute housewife might abide. I can't recommend visiting, I'm afraid.

Anyway. Late on an April afternoon, Maggie walked along Front Street, bound for the butcher's to acquire a chop for her husband and scraps for her Labrador, when a rumpled, hairy figure lurched from the shadows and struck the back of her head with a bowling pin. This was George Silva, an Azorean baker, who mistook Maggie for his wife; he had been drinking bathtub wine all day in the alley beside his shop, and everyone looked like everyone else, more or less, in their shapeless black coats and big hats and long scarves. Mrs. Silva had taken up

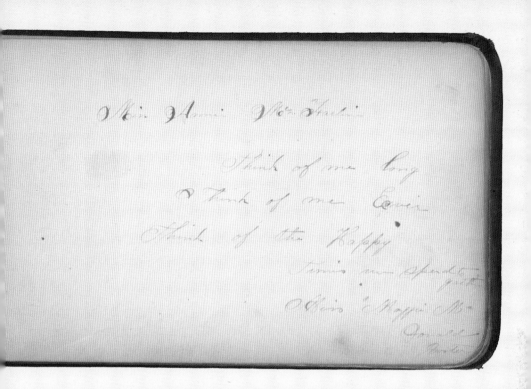

with another gentleman, and George's response to the situation was not measured, not cosmopolitan, although having never been cuck-olded myself, I have no basis for judging the tenor of his reaction. Why and where from a bowling pin, I can't imagine. Maggie, skull crushed, in a slurry of cranial fluid and teeth, died before the doctor arrived. George was briefly restrained by passersby, but escaped their hold and fled across the village green and into the woods; he was found dead in New Hampshire, drowned in a quarry, eight months later. A cousin, by the way, was Maggie McDonald: Andrew McFarlane's sister's daughter. Her direct descendants are as dead as she.

To Annie

When twilight draws your curtain
down and pins it with a star remember
your fond friend though she may
                              wander far
                Your fond friend
                Mary McDonald
                Vanceboro
                    Maine

From July 1887 until June 1888, the McFarlanes attempted to make of their Vanceboro, Maine residence a permanent home. Andrew had enjoyed several lucrative years, and very much liked the idea of becoming a country squire. He had grand ideas for expanding their property: a guest wing, a carriage house, a new lawn for bowling and croquet, a tennis court, an English garden, statues of Roman emperors, et cetera. The bracing properties of the northern wind, and the medicinal balsam upon it, would harden his lungs and restore his diminished bedchamber energies. For the children, there was a not-bad girls' academy nearby: the Vanceboro School, the kind of place well-bred people send their wayward ones, and ill-bred people send their smart ones, and everyone is uplifted by the wonders of nature and hard work. And a substantial Francophone community contained plenty of widows who, for a handful of buffalo nickels, could elevate the young ladies' speech with charming fragments of French, *comme tous les meilleurs singes bourgeois.*

The harshness of the winter was not adequately considered: the family was snowed in for weeks at a time, and Andrew acquired frostbite on the tip of his nose while searching in the frozen dusk for Achilles, Annie's marmalade tom, who was later found sleeping in a linens cabinet. Neither was the substantial population of bachelor lumber-jacks who worked a nearby camp, always lingering outside the general store, the tavern, livid with sexual menace. Nor the low standards of the housekeepers and the cooks available, always muttering as they simulated dusting, or as they boiled without seasoning another skinny chicken. Nor the meanness and crudity of the local craftsmen, who overcharged for all their slapdash work—the uneven bookshelves, the screaming doors—and who mocked Andrew's dressing gown and co-lognes, and who cursed and spat in front of women. Staid Boston's permanent cold shoulder felt, upon the family's return, like the most fevered, bosomy embrace.

Mary McDonald—well, reader, there are so many Mary McDonalds in the world. Select, from their gibbering pile, one of the many Mary McDonalds you already know, and project her onto this one. It's what you would have done anyway.

[14r]

Dear Annie,

Remember thy Creator
In the days of thy youth.

Mrs. James E. Kelly

St. Croix[?]
Feb 24/88

St. Croix, here, refers not to the delightful Caribbean island—why, reader, would it?—but to Vanceboro's Canadian twin, across the St. Croix River. It's a village as undistinguished as Vanceboro, though with that subtle surplus of order and restraint—smoother roads, tidier homes, healthier trees—you expect from Canada, stereotypes being stereotypes because of their essential truth. Put it this way: in St. Croix, a girl might worry about birthing an imbecile because she, like her mother and grandmother, married her first cousin; in Vanceboro, a girl might worry about birthing an imbecile because she was raped by the semiverbal clod who collects scrap wood for spare pennies and plates of beans and lives in a shed behind the sawmill.

Mrs. James Kelly—Myrna—assisted in the chapel at the Vanceboro School, where she organized drawers of tapers, hung up the many silks, wrote to catalogs for incense, erased dirty words penciled in hymnals. Her husband, a potato farmer, had died some winters earlier, cause unknown; the records of this era, of this region, are neither detailed nor well kept—think of flashlights in humid cellars, facefuls of musty spores. Their son, a shipping clerk in Halifax, encouraged Myrna to join his household there, but she was stubborn, and possessed that unendearing but nevertheless quite common sense that

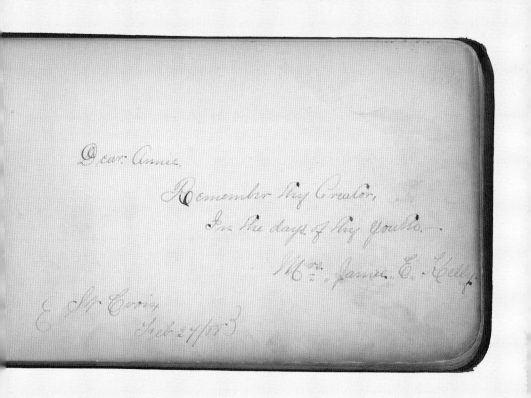

Dear Annie,

Remember Thy Creator,
In the days of thy youth.—

Mrs. James E. Kelly

E. St. Croix
Feb 27/03

an omniscient someone, or a bureau of someones, all wearing dons' gowns and carrying clipboards in their extradimensional academy, measured her suffering, her loneliness, her martyrdom, chalking scores on a slate, calculating them, recording them in a vast ledger, ranking her against the rest of Christian humanity. But expend no sympathy, please, as pathetic as this seems. This is a repugnant habit. A selfish habit. No one feels fine—I don't, and neither do you. All is an ordeal, and pride is the first resort of small minds.

I found Myrna's gravestone half-hidden by tall grass and eroded about its edges, its inscription obscured by moss and blue-green mold. No flowers—for her or her neighboring corpses. Lots of mosquitoes and black flies. The dull sunlight was muddy and ocher-tinged, filtered through low, wet clouds that rippled mere inches above the pitch pines and the aspens.

To Annie

When Sailing down the River of life
In your little Bark canoe
May you have a pleasant trip
With Just Room enough for two

your cousin

August 19th
1888

H H Mills

Oh, another vague cousin—maternal, second, once removed. Helen Honoria Mills was, in her youth, of a feisty bohemian type, adopting defiantly certain habits of the stronger sex—hair-chopping, whiskey-drinking, pistol-shooting, breeches-wearing, chaw-spitting —though by her late twenties the effort required to keep up such appearances, and the inconvenience of the resulting social exclusion, and her brother's threats of disinheritance, led her back to the realms of corsetry, enormous dresses, and hats laden with feathers and silk roses. Her suppressed instincts she diverted into a mania for physical vigor and enthusiasm for the outdoors. She was the first woman to climb every peak of New Hampshire's Presidential Range, and the first woman to be admitted to the South End Dumbbell Club. She swam from Fort Point to Winthrop in record time—a feat made even more impressive by her impractical, nonaerodynamic, though modest, so modest, bathing costume. She chopped her own wood and shoveled her own coal, to the merriment of astonished passersby.

In the summer of 1884 Helen paddled the length of the Connecticut River in a birchbark canoe that she had constructed under the supervision of John Sauvage, a supposed Abenaki shaman; the journey was recounted in *Algonquin Evenings*, a well-reviewed if little-read travel-

[14v]

To Annie

When sailing down the river of life
In your little bark canoe
May you have a pleasant trip
With just room enough for two

Your cousin
H. H. Mills

August 19th
1888

ogue in which the tension between her disdain for mills and dams, and her dependence upon, and delight in, their productions, presaged the queasy pieties of later generations. Still, the book got her invited to cocktail parties in New York, and her witty, eccentric performances there, coupled with the pleasant tenor of her prose, gained her diverting assignments from newspapers and magazines. She toured the jungles of the Maya for *Fowler's Monthly*. She interviewed Sitting Bull for the *Illustrated News*. She reviewed more or less any narrative work written by a woman, for anyone willing to pay. The money wasn't terrible, and neither were the cocktails.

Helen shared rooms on Lime Street in Boston with Elisa Jane Ashburn, the painter, with whom she enjoyed a *perfectly chaste* relationship until their simultaneous deaths in 1910 (malfunctioning furnace, carbon monoxide).

[15r]

To Annie

When you are sitting all alone
In some pleasant spot
Just pluck that little flower
The sweet forgetme not.

R. McDonald

Forget-me-nots are frail blue flowers easily mistaken for blooming weeds. Were they in my yard, had I a yard and no caretaker for it, I would assault them with rakes and poisons. I don't see why they're any nicer than dandelions or poison oak. (Poison oak is rather alluring—that waxy, opalescent shine, like the surface of a soap bubble.) The idea, I suppose, is that forget-me-nots are wildflowers readily accessed for plucking by girls gone off into nature—a rolling meadow, the bank beside a whispering creek, a grove of willows whose profuse green curtain screens one's tears from the eyes of the public—for sessions of distant gazes and wistful sighs. Adolescent women are prone to this, I understand, or were in earlier eras, when they were still expected to regulate their desires. A healthier state, this. Desire leads one to, if not ruin, or not inevitably ruin, then to the shattering of many sustaining illusions. The shards, spread so wide and in such small, transparent pieces, escape the broom, the vacuum, embedded, as they are, between floorboards and in the weave of carpets, wounding bare feet for indefinite years. Restraint bestows a holy glory, anyhow. One faces the world lit by its radiance, with dramatic, handsome shadows cast. It's Hollywood-terrific.

To Annie

When you are sitting all alone
In some pleasant spot
Just pluck that little flower
The sweet forget-me-not.

R. McDonald

Richard McDonald, a ginger-haired, flushed-faced, plump, pig-nosed boy, lived in the neighborhood, in a drafty but fetching Georgian on John Street. Despite his savage appearance—he looked as if he should be stealing pennies from the eyes of corpses in a Belfast slum—Richard was a bright, polite boy, attending Roxbury Latin, writing precocious essays after the manner of his idol, Oliver Wendell Holmes, and playing Falstaff to blustering perfection in the Roslindale Young Players' production of *Henry IV, Part I*. His promise meant nothing—it rarely does, haven't you noticed? Richard acquired tuberculosis and, despite taking cold-weather treatments at Iroquois Mountain, an Adirondack sanitarium, and adopting a vegetarian diet centered upon boiled spinach and cereal grains, died a month before his nineteenth birthday, beneath a drenched calico quilt, surrounded by spine-bent volumes of Stoic philosophy, his notebooks of poems and anatomical drawings of gulls, his bloody handkerchiefs, his pails of sputum.

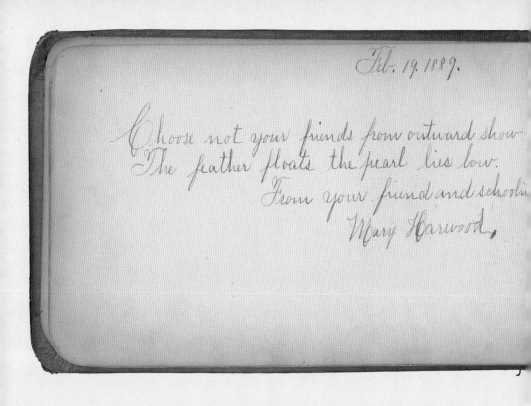

Feb. 19. 1889.

Choose not your friends from outward show
The feather floats the pearl lies low.
From your friend and schoolm[...]
Mary Harwood,

Mary Harwood married Joseph Baker, a baker, in 1903, and birthed a Joseph Junior, a Sarah, a Brian, a Ralph, and a Bernard, all of whom—save for Brian, who saw some success as a railroad attorney—evaporated into laboring obscurity. She died in 1967 of ischemia, at Faulkner Hospital, Boston, and there's the extent of her public record. One expects that she rode in trolleys and buses and later private cars, prayed in churches, cooked Sunday roasts, purchased hats and bonnets and pinned carnations to her bosom, on humid days applied talc to her body's many crevices, abhorred profane language, felt relieved by her husband's early passing, and filled her teacup with whiskey each night after everyone else had gone to bed. Nevertheless, Mary Harwood might as well not have existed—or might well not have existed, like a transitional hominid implied by the fossil record, but for which no bones can be found.

In one of those coincidences that serve to remind one that the world is tiny and cruel, and that its creator possesses, among His unsavory traits, a fallow imagination, I find that I briefly attended high school with Mary's great-granddaughter, the poetess Charlene Alt, who was two forms my senior at Saint Simon's School. We didn't associate—I never associate—but I remember, I think, that she roomed in

[15v]

Feb. 19. 1989.

Choose not your friends from outward show
The feather floats the pearl lies low.

From your friend and schoolmate
Mary Harwood

the Tudor turret of Tarbox Hall, that she was suspended for smoking, and—yes—her disconcerting eyes, the irises of which were so dark that they could not be distinguished from her pupils. Charlene now chairs the Department of Creative Writing at an agricultural college near Fort Lauderdale, and from this humid perch dispenses unceasing reams of well-praised free verse, all dense with images of tumescent reptiles and demonic father-lovers. Her work has appeared in *Authority Bulletin* and the *Prismatic Review*, and she is a recipient of both the John Francis Queeny Award and the Rector of Freiburg's Prize in Poetry. One day the entire state of Florida will be under eighteen feet of water, and I shall not realize the difference.

[16r]

Fall from a steeple
Fall from above
Fall from anywhere
But don't fall in love

Susie McLaughlin

Jan. 14. 1889.

Susie—bright-eyed and mostly pretty in her pictures, save for an unfortunate forehead (so tall!) and an odd curvature in her jaw—offers useful advice. I fell in love with both of my wives and so was blind to their defects (priggishness, prudishness, frigidity, rapacity, improvidence, belligerence, venality—and so on, reader, so, so on). With Naomi, my first wife, I was young enough never to question the desire of another when that desire coincided with my own. A common error: I just had the misfortune of making it legally binding. With my second wife, Mariel, there are no such excuses. Despite my pretensions of wisdom, of stoic control, I remain susceptible to flattery and appetite, and wondered not enough—not at all, somehow—why such a fetching creature, fifteen years my junior, seven thousand miles away, pursued me so recklessly, or how she might have found my several social media profiles in the first place. The thrust and bearing of that plot ought to have been transparent.

Consequences? Naomi is still nourished by the sweet nectar of my financial fruit: I cover, as I earlier alluded, two-thirds of her mortgage payment, and bestow a further sum once per quarter, and she is kept in her faux-bohemian splendor. With Mariel the arrangement is more informal, indeed is in most respects a bribe: a demand is com-

Fall from a steeple
Fall from above
Fall from anywhere
But don't fall in love
                    Susie McLaughlin
Jan 14 1889

municated, I enact a wire transfer, and in exchange she remains in Cebu City, living like a soap opera queen on her walled estate, and promises, for at least another several months, to book no trans-Pacific flights, to heave hither and tither, to curious attorneys and police, no more untidy, untrue accusations. I suffer an urge to evacuate my bowels when oversized designer sunglasses are balanced atop a woman's head. Shopping malls repulse me, particularly the high-end sorts with valets and dining concepts by celebrity chefs. When I see a fresh-faced lad promenading with his girl—worse, with his girl and a stroller—one part of me wishes to cry, and another to drain my accounts buying him a false identity and a one-way ticket for the Argentine Pampas. Poor sperm motility is a secret blessing.

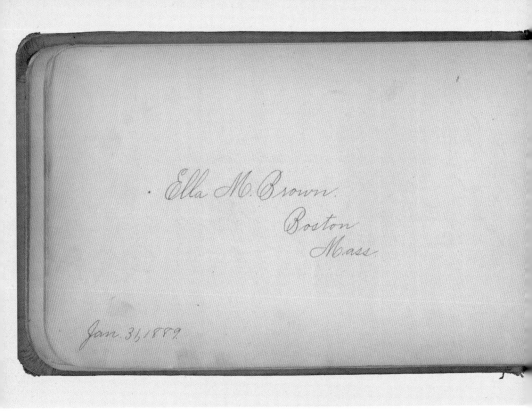

Ella Brown, another schoolmate, and perhaps the worst yet. A pert, weasel-like face; a flat bony chest; a long neck mounted precariously atop concrete shoulders. Her marks were poor. She never did her assigned reading—perhaps she couldn't at all; I have no proof otherwise, so let us assume. She unclogged her ears with dull pencils—how the other girls loved to ape this when Ella's back was turned, holding any pencil-shaped object, a finger if nothing funnier came to hand, and twisting it vigorously by their own ears while gritting their teeth or projecting their tongues and rolling up their eyes ecstatically, epileptically. She once destroyed the school canteen with a fire started while attempting to boil a kettle. Nevertheless, upon graduating high school, Ella married Peter Greenfield, a temperate, wanly handsome bookbinder with a little bit of family money. Despite their legal and cultural advantages, men of the era were desperate to wed. They twisted themselves like palsied contortionists into grotesque, unnatural shapes, that they might fit into the cubbies and footlockers and behind-the-staircase nooks in which they were compelled to store themselves. This isn't to say the same thing doesn't happen now—but you expect it, don't you, in such a culture as ours, where boys are made eunuchs of the spirit before adolescence, the shades of their testes left to rot like gibbeted murderers along our roadsides and in our town squares. What a hash was made of patriarchy.

Ella and Peter had however many children they had, lived however long they lived in whatever place they lived, died whenever they died—you get it. A couple of names on a headstone somewhere. Adjacent headstones etched with similarly unexciting surnames, all unadorned marble—the entry headstone models all around, I'm sure. Brown petals on a wind-ripped wreath. A miniature American flag, made of synthetic cloth by Indonesian child laborers, planted in the uneven dirt, because some dead cretin served in whatever war, slaughtering whomever to preserve the security of global capital. The jagged fragments of liquor bottles smashed by trite teens. Cemeteries—I don't know about cemeteries. I prefer the Parsi method of exposing one's corpse atop a tower for the delectation of ravens and crows. The odor must be severe. I suppose they burn some rich native shrub to mask it.

Annie

All common things, each day's events
That with the hour begin and end
Our pleasures and our discontents
Are rounds by which we may ascend

Very Truly Your Friend
Ida L. Dobb
Vanceboro

June. 1888.

That's a bit of Longfellow: a dreadful bit of Longfellow. A banal sentiment, a language, and a rhythm all as musty as root cellars, as unchallenging as games of checkers. It's no wonder he was, and remains, a favorite of children, the senile, and New Englanders. The moon-eyed, tin-eared twerp.

The daughter of a country judge, Ida graduated from the Vanceboro School, spent a half-year taking brief, nauseated glances at the required materials of the freshman curriculum at Mount Holyoke, then returned home to look after the office of her father, Erasmus Dobb, a judge of the Maine Superior Court. She was engaged to a Portland lawyer, but found herself charmed, and soon impregnated, by a horse-car operator and trade unionist called Eugene Szabo. Szabo, a brawny figure with a long, wicked mustache, was subject to surveillance and frequent beatings by agents of the Portland Railroad Company, and the city police. This spices a marriage as a dash of Tabasco does a plate of eggs. Every lady loves to suture a hero's wounds. Ida raised nine children in a Parkside triple-decker apartment that smelled of garlic and boiled linens. Nine children of one's own, my god. I can scarcely tolerate a single child, seated on the opposite side of a restaurant. The unmodulated volume of his shrill voice, his baths of saliva and slurped

Annie

All common things, each day's events
That with the hour begin & end
Our pleasures & our discontents
Are rounds by which we may ascend

Very Truly Your Friend
Ida L. Cobb

June. 1888.   Vanceboro

mucus. His insipid crayon drawings, which display no promise whatsoever, but for which we all must feign our appreciation. The assault of his gaze and lisped interrogation when his arrogant parent permits him to wander. No tips are dispensed on these occasions, and I am unable to finish my meal. The bill is hastily paid, and I retire to the men's room to reassure myself with liberal applications of liquid soap. So, no, none for me, try as my wives might have. I've debated purchasing a surgical assurance, but I fear such would make me feel too unmanned. And you always worry, or I always worry, anyway, about inheriting an unexpected title of nobility; I should hate to be known as the ball-less last Marquess of Lydney, or what have you, in the merciless tabloids.

A neighborhood girl—mother dead, father a construction foreman often away, toothless watery-eyed grandmother imported from Silesia to brine meats and murmur obscurely over a Polish Bible. An avid reader of riddle books and cowboy stories. Fond of ribbons, and pinching lengths of silk between her thumb and forefinger. Always beat Annie at jacks. Played a nasty viola—no, never in tune, never. Bright white skin, the color of new plaster, that flushed unalluringly after exercise like the scales of a blotchy carp. Carp: she liked to eat this, in aspic, on Christmas Eve. Though willowy in youth, she widened once mature, accreting mass like a planetisimal, all aswirl in stellar dust and apple crumble, until she attracted satellites, diverted comets, tipped benches, required two seats on trains. Attended Mass twice a week despite professing a sense of God's indifference to her presence, and her doubts as to the purity and good intentions of the Church as a social entity. Voted Democratic in every election despite professing her sense of the party's indifference to her support, and her doubts as to the purity and good intentions of the party as a representative of her social class. Uncomfortable with the pace of racial integration; moved house from Hyde Park to Dedham Square after a colored family purchased the saltbox twelve doors down. Disciplined

Sarah Klatschkey
Boston
Mass.

her children with the blank of her husband's fly rod. An octagonal mole on her left cheek acquired, as she aged, a violet hue. The blond hairs above her lip became interspersed with long black ones—brittle things prone to split ends and possessing no follicle when plucked. Ankles like dock posts. Toenails like pistachio shells. Owned hundreds of silk kerchiefs, most of them patterned with images of tropical fruits or of songbirds. Owned one negligee, cream-colored, with a water-stain at the hip. In widowhood acquired an autographed photo of Zane Grey, which she framed and mounted to the wall above her bed, beneath the iron crucifix. I could do this all day, though I'd rather not.

Boston Jan. 17, 1889

When you are alone, Smashing dishes,
Remember me with the best of wishes.

Your Loving Friend
Katie M. Reardon
Boston
Mass

Jan. 17, 1889.

While dish-smashing was never Annie's preferred method of express-
ing displeasure—the virtue of thrift stood paramount in her mind,
when chastity failed to provide a more immediate advantage—Katie's
sentiment is not misplaced. Famous, in family lore, were the Christmas roast thrown to the floor for the retrievers, the album of photographs set ablaze, the razor streaked across the portrayed neck of an
elder Dawes's oil portrait. These acts were triggered by the most banal
remarks imaginable—or if not the *most* banal, remarks at which you
or I, reader, would merely incline our heads, then shrug and sip our
coffee or cordial, if we observed them at all: a request for salt, noting a
draft or another's fine dress. Such was Annie's way, though such ways
are only pardonable if you're very rich or very beautiful, and she was,
as you know, neither. Her destructive imprint has lingered for generations, driving our male line to make disastrous romantic choices. I'm
skint because of it, and fortunate to have avoided castration by Pinoy
gangsters. My father *was* castrated, spiritually, anyhow. His phantom
manhood was kept for many years, bronzed or preserved in a liquid
suspension, as I imagine it, in Taos, on a shelf that overlooked the
blue-tiled hot tub where my mother entertained hordes of frolicsome
Navajos. Dad did grow back his apparatus, in time, though in a com-

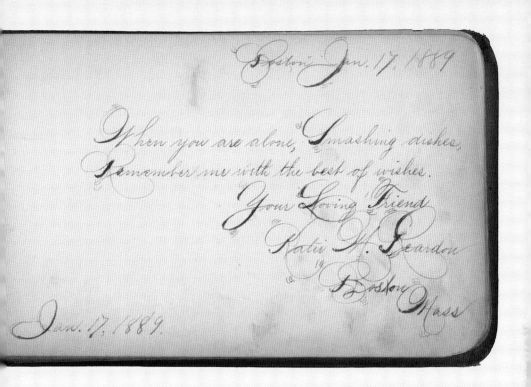

Boston Jan. 17, 1889

When you are alone, Smashing dishes,
Remember me with the best of wishes.
Your Loving Friend
Katie H. Reardon
Boston Mass

Jan. 17, 1889.

promised state—a wee machine the size of, as fragile as, a humming-bird's egg, the pulleys and pivots and gears inside prone to jams and in need of frequent lubrication—and its reduced energetic output is directed nowadays at performing violent yard work and shouting at golf tournaments on television.

Katie Reardon's penmanship resembles the girl herself: oversized, with decorative flourishes she's incapable of pulling off. A blob of black silk, English lace, and furs, she broke, I suppose, many dishes of her own—and many chairs—with John Wesley, the architect, whom she married in 1895, and whose acquaintance with advanced mathematics and the principles of engineering enabled him to father Katie's four children. Their great-grandson, Jeremy Wesley, is a fixture on the northeastern folk circuit, treating Unitarian basements from Hoboken to Halifax to his plaintive mandolin and hushed baritone and words of wind and the sea. His beard, like his belly, is enormous.

"Donahoe" is a variation of "Donahue." The latter, you'll agree, is more common, and more pleasing to the ear, and on the tongue. More pleasing, too, in the brain. "Donahue" is an apple-cheeked charmer, dancing in pubs, playing plaintive melodies on penny whistles, buying you drinks. "Donahoe" is a black-eyed clod with dirt on his fingers, always short of coin and credit, always puking in a gutter; you can smell the waste waft, and the sticky maple of his diabetes. Both names—along with their many siblings—are derived from the Gaelic *Donnchadh*, meaning, more or less, "dun-colored cow." The ancient family was known in Kerry for its expansive herds. This wealth evaporated during the Tudor dynasty, and we thereafter witness a succession of gaunt cottars lazing against half-ruined drystone walls, amid all the unmolested heather.

Let's pity, then, poor Mamie, a codependent with scarce chances—at beauty, brains, attainment, anything. Island genetics cursed her with paper-thin, paper-white skin, chaotic teeth, a figure like an ill-maintained column of juniper, and a mind predisposed to unproductive rumination. The meager exposure provided by her education at the Pickard School, which was not exactly the society grooming-house it dreamed itself to be, nor the polisher of intellects, further slashed at

[18v]

To Annie

If rocks and rills divied us
And you I cannot see
Remember it was Mamie
That wrote these lines.

Your True Friend
Mamie Donahoe

January, 30, 1889.

For.   Get   Me   Not

---

her moorings. In the face of privilege, however shambling and provisional that privilege may be, the natural reaction of the unworthy is to drift, drift through thin atmosphere, to suffocate in vacuum. There are diversions, but those such as Mamie who lack an appetite for pleasure will find no recourse—for them, only anxiety and impoverishment remain, like winter winds blowing the cobwebs from a ruined amphitheater's collapsed columns. It's a wonder, and some kind of testament, I guess, that she didn't kill herself, and survived, silent and alone with her tabloids and supper trays, in the spare bedroom of her brother's house, until a cancer of the stomach overtook her. Three points to Catholicism, if you still have your scorecard.

[19r]

"To Annie"

When your husband at you fling
Knives, Forks and other things
Seek relief and seek it soon
In the handle of the Broom

Your loving Friend
Bertha Nason

Love your enemy

M.H.

"Love your enemy," notes M.H., May Horton, in the margin. Love even Bertha Nason. "Bertha Nason": such a corpulent archaism. One imagines vast bloomers flown like royal banners on the laundry line, and a fetid sweat masked with baby powder. In fact Bertha was of an average build—perhaps even slender, beneath the scrapheap of Victorian cloths into which she and her contemporaries burrowed themselves, who knows—and fetching enough, in a wide-faced, monochromatic, half-Polish way. Her only physical flaws worthy of noting were an emphatic jaw—the strength of which some, yours truly included, would deem a sensual provocation—and her enormous calves. I mean, outrageous calves: like powder kegs, or redwood stumps. (A redwood is visible through the window of my present lodging, planted in the verge that divides the parking lot from the boulevard, ringed by fecal mulch and blonde tufts of feather grass. It's a sickly representative, its needles gone pale, its bark mottled and half-peeled, like an old banana. A telephone pole might furnish a sheerer beauty.) Gentlemen were charmed by Bertha, which always galls the charmless. Annie was charmless. This we know, and so well. "Love your enemy." Annie couldn't quite get to this, and settled for loving enemies. She kept them as a less awful person keeps cats: to stroke, to feed, to caress

"To Annie"

"When your husband at you fling
Knives. Forks and other things
Seek relief and seek it soon
In the handle of the Broom

Your loving Friend
Bertha Nason

in the dark. Bertha, yes, was the dreaded figure of 1889 into whose plush effigy pins were lustily thrust. To subsequent fores in subsequent years came Francine Donlan, Mildred Brattle, Paulette Fonesca, Irene Brooks, Goldie Fowler, Jeanette Forbes, Josephine O'Connell, Louise Parker, Anne Scerra, Geraldine Fitzmiller, Ellen Margosian, Bonnie Ballard, Rhonda Cooke, Carla Hrbosky, Gertrude Cornwallis, Mildred Walsh, Agnes Walsh, Lenora Walsh, Esther Biddle, Claire Engel, Justine Van Klaven, Lauren McBride, Susanne Clark, and Donna Feldman. There are letters I've recovered whose tart, terse prose and pressured handwriting suggest a subterranean nastiness, seams of sulfurous groundwater all aboil, seams of coal afire, the churn of magma. The letters also contain a colorful assortment of racial and religious epithets, a number of them so novel, or sufficiently antiquated, to have surprised and amused your diligent researcher. My convulsions, as I laughed, nearly tore the brittle, musty, dusty pages between my fingers.

The McFarlanes' housekeeper at Vanceboro, Maud Landry, was an iron-haired, tomato-faced character of no distinction, as you ought to have expected. I expect she was permitted to apply this autograph out of a grim liberal sympathy—the stubby pencil gripped by stubby, barnacled fingers—with the hardships of the working classes. Overfamiliar tears were secreted upon the McFarlanes' return to Boston, and poor Maud moved back to her drafty cabin, and resumed her lonely suppers of fatback and wild blueberries.

I have a nervous relationship with housekeepers, myself. Although fastidious in my hygiene—my inheritance, this—all is never just right, and something mortifying is left to sully their paid hands. A bath towel with an alarming stain. Pubic hairs upon the rim of the toilet and the sink. Catsup on the counterpane. Forgotten, fragrant underclothes. My embarrassment at these, and at my expectation that remedying them should be the responsibility of another, is compounded by the fact that I find so many housekeepers so bewitching. The strong, dusky ladies. An old-fashioned predilection, but there it is. A ruffled apron, a pair of rubber gloves, cords of muscle all tensed, the scent of ammonia on the air: across this ground runs the highway to desire, paved in sparkling marble, lined by fountains in which Win-

[19v]

Don't forget your Friend
Maud
Vanceboro
Maine

dex and Drano brightly arc. If only I owned the means to pay its many tolls. Though I possess some facility with the written word, I am a bumbler with the spoken, should remarks have gone unprepared. One inquires brightly after the health of their children, should they own any, and at the states of their romantic attachments. Spurred by their disengaged response, one stumbles into an imitation English-Spanish pidgin, manufactured from restaurant menus and accents in comic films. Suddenly another room requires attention, or the vacuum must be engaged. I understand. My deepest apologies to all the beautiful, diligent women whom I've terrified. It was always unwitting, I promise, and I love you.

Annie

May you always
Remain the same
In everything
Except your name

Your Friend
Emily Cobb.

Vanceboro Maine June 7th 1888

A daughter of J. Endicott Cobb, the steelmaker, Emily's early education was in the hands of untested governesses, who treated her as a friendly, sentient doll; and at nine she was sent away to the Lemuel School in remotest Pennsylvania, the first of a dozen boarding schools attended in a peripatetic academic career. By the time she arrived at Vanceboro, Emily knew all the best, newest, louchest card games, could play on the piano popular tunes both heartbreaking and ribald, kept bottles of Madeira in a hidden compartment of her steamer trunk, and was well informed about the acquisition and use of French purses—she was just wayward enough, in other words, to be more interesting than everyone else without tipping into vulgarity. What exerted balance were her excellent manners, New York urbanity, careless trill of a laugh, and elegant, fine-boned, china-white face. Had she been impoverished, obese, a dowd, or had she possessed a Mediterranean unibrow or a mole like a bonbon, her quirks of personality would have rendered her a figure of curious amusement at best, and at worst one as indecorous, and as unworthy, as the desperate old tart who dances in states of undress for hurled nickels behind stained curtains at a carnival. Good looks smooth the surface of the roughest

Annie

May you always
Remain the same
In everything
Except your name

Your Friend
Emily Cott.

Vanceboro Maine June 7th 1885.

plane. Money then coats it with an industrial lubricant to which nothing clings.

Emily married an Austrian prince whose conduct in the first war was sufficiently indifferent for his estates to have been left intact, and who had the foresight to divest himself of his assets and move the proceeds to Switzerland in the early Thirties, during the Dolfuss regime. There occurred a splendid late life, untroubled by war or privation, enjoying Alpine slopes and flowering meadows, attended by sturdy, loyal retainers of the old school (the last of their kind), surrounded by children and grandchildren, who married and diffused themselves into the cream of the continent: a Danish princess, a Romanov, a Scottish laird and his cousin the Irish baron, an awkward but absurdly wealthy Italian tycoon. And Emily still thought to send Annie a telegram of consolation upon the death of Charles Dawes. Brief, but still. Still!

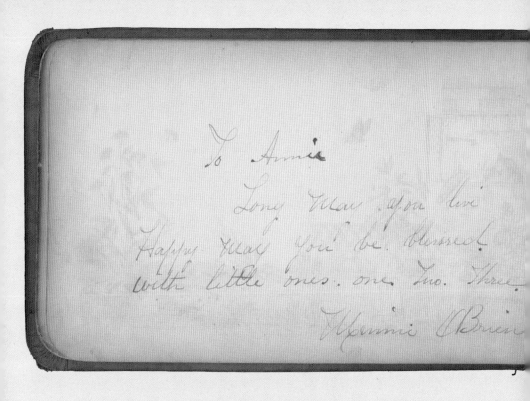

To Annie

Long May you live
Happy May you be. blessed
with little ones. one. Two. Three.

Mennie O'Brien

I have been unable to identify this Mennie O'Brien. I'm not even certain what sort of name is "Mennie"; short for something, surely, but
I lack data, and desire, to guess for what it may be a diminutive. The
handwriting looks elderly. The surname suggests a paternal relation
or a domestic servant. A withered old cousin or aunt? A cook? The
silver-buffer?

Annie conceived but a single child, my grandfather, Thomas Andrew Dawes, who himself managed but one, my father, Edward Arthur
Dawes, of whom yours truly is the sole (known) offspring. We Dawes
men are not prolific in our breeding. We are also prone to diabetes
and pulmonary complaints. My grandfather had chronically occluded
veins and, late in his life, a wet brain. My father was excused from military service because of the delicacy of the bones in his feet, and his
spectacles are eight inches thick. I have a weak chin, a weak jaw, and
am thus forced to wear a beard, despite its intractable kinks and flak-
ing and sparse patches; it resembles that of a mountaineer returned
half-frozen and malnourished from an exploration of the Turkestani
Massif in which his supply train was buried by a gorge's collapsing
face and all of his attendants were eaten by snow leopards. My earwax
must be periodically vacuumed by medical professionals. It would

be in bad taste to begin a discussion of our heritable psychological impediments.

With all luck the family line terminates with me—my ghostly terminal, an empty station in a derelict neighborhood, full of shattered windows, powdered masonry, pigeon roosts, overflowed sewage, heroin galleries, and the open fires of squatting indigents. On the crumbling platforms, ancient maps, peeling from their boards, water-stained, streaked with bird shit, text illegible, display tangles of color marking routes long abandoned, the past's infinitely expansive service. I await the wrecking balls and bulldozers. So far, so good. Despite two wives and a latex allergy, I have not engendered. I am unprepared, at this point, to enter into any further sexual, or even companionable, relationship. I have difficult standards that must be met; I must be cautious around matters of finance; and time has become so scarce—or rather, I have become so conscious of its scarcity. You would think a clearly demarcated end to suffering would relieve a fellow, but how wrong, how wrong.

To Annie;—

Some may wish the happiness,
Some others may wish the wealth,
My wish is better far,
Contentment blessed
With health.

Your loving friend,
Mary Hughes

For-get-me-not.

Although we briefly find Mary's note uplifting—it's nice to see a girl who dreams of *being okay*, rather than of husbands and jewelry and teeming broods—consideration tears the sentiment into threads of useless fluff. Ignore her odd grammar, which I assume results from an excess of haste, along with her, oh, "rugged" metrical decisions. What's the difference between happiness and contentment? I should think them the same thing, separated only by degrees—that is, contentment is a mild form of happiness, happiness a heightened contentment. Is this not correct? Does it matter if it's not correct? Both are fleeting—fleeing—specters, scraps of fog negligently anthropomorphized. One pursues each, either, and never catches up. The horizon is always the horizon, and moves with you. One might stumble upon them, true, in a remote cavern, a chateau's attic, an abandoned museum annex, and share for a while their space, but seek to grasp them and one's hands pass right through, one's body heat speeds their evaporation. And these spectral fogs are transparent—even if one encounters such a mass of the stuff that one's view is consumed, the world behind is never blotted out, is always shimmering there, waiting, imposing its permanence. Millionaires and yogic masters might construct psychic devices that allow such clouds to

To Annie;—
Some may wish the happiness,
Some other may wish the wealth,
My wish is better far,
Contentment bless
With health.
Your loving friend
Mary Hughes

Forget-me-not

be captured and condensed, stored and accessed as found useful or pleasing, and perhaps could immerse themselves in sealed chambers of the steamy material, as if taking a *schvitz*. The leisure of the untroubled mind. The untroubled mind of leisure.

The illustration is a delight, at which I should like to cry.

Mary was a third cousin to Charles Evans Hughes, the candidate, cabinet secretary, and chief justice. They met a mere handful of times, but she once kissed his well-trimmed cheek at a holiday party, an incident that she would incessantly recollect, to anyone nearby, whenever his name appeared in the morning's *Globe*, or was spoken on the wireless.

"Be good, sweet maid, and let who will
    be clever,
Do noble things, not dream them all
    day long;
And so make life, death and that va[st]
    forever
One grand sweet song."

                        Mary A. Mitehill

March 15 1889.

Mary Mitehill—another Mary, my god—was the daughter of Colonel Gregory Stearnes Mitehill, an army figure of note. Commissioned as a second lieutenant in 1862, he rose swiftly in rank, carried by his relentless stamina—he slept, like Napoleon, four hours each night—and his diligent, mathematical approach to the application of violence. He claimed to have taken the mortal shot that felled Quantrill himself, of Quantrill's Raiders, though there is every reason to doubt his veracity on the matter; a dozen other men in the ambush party made the same claim. He claimed further to have slain Quantrill's second in command, the notorious Caleb Todd, in a dramatic bout of swashbuckling combat, in the end disemboweling him with a stray cavalry saber stuck fortuitously in an adjacent hay bale. A war saber was indeed mounted above Colonel Mitehill's Beacon Hill fireplace, and black stains of oxidized blood and viscera did remain visible on its blade; but the Colonel, as his household was obliged to call him, was not tidy—he always left crumbs on the tablecloth, and dribbled his tea, and lost buttons on his waistcoat—and he killed so many people. Dispatched westward to help tame the plains in April 1869, Mitehill commanded operations at Fort Pope in the Dakota Territory, where he ordered the razing of a half-dozen Sioux and Cheyenne encampments, and

[partially effaced] To

"Be good, sweet maid, and let who will
be clever,
Do noble things, not dream them all
day long:
And so make life, death and that vast
forever
One grand sweet song."

Mary A. Mitehill.

March 15. 1889.

---

personally hanged fifteen Sioux raiders. He resigned his commission in March 1870, having found the winter weather intolerable, its cold temperatures and incessant wind aggravated by the absence of civilized comforts—drinkable liquors, continental cooking, opera halls, bathing salts, a fleshly wife. Settling in Boston, in his childhood home, a redbrick town house on Beacon Hill that he had at some point inherited, the Colonel attempted careers as a memoirist and playwright, failing at each; he stood for the legislature and the Board of Alderman time and again, and was never elected; he joined the boards of several manufacturing enterprises, all of which failed. But he had his substantial inheritance, and was still invited to noteworthy parties and suppers, and treated at them with his due deference, at least to his furry face. An 1886 photo portrait displays the Colonel's rich mustache, a silky, shining monster of an affectation, curled flawlessly about his lips like a panther basking.

Mary Mitehill married the son of a well-known grocer and played in bridge games with Annie, off and on, until she died of a pulmonary embolism, 1946.

To Annie

He who clothes the lilies
And marks the sparrows fall
Protect and save you Annie
And keep you safe thro' all

Your Schoolmate
Dottie Rhodes

Jan 14, 1888.

Dottie was the niece of Clarence Mudie, whose signature and note you recall. An adroit tennis player and pianist, with auburn hair done in cascades of tight lustrous curls. Dottie's face contained a blur of freckles of which she was rightly ashamed; rather than the ornaments of a Hibernian scamp, they resembled symptoms of a tropical disease. I am repulsed by conditions of the skin. Pox, melanomas, psoriatic lesions: my belly quakes, my throat seizes. If my waiter has an oversized or irregular mole, or a minor cut or scrape visible, even a shaving nick, back to the kitchen goes my soup course, uneaten, and my bill is promptly settled, and out, out I flee, into—I pray into—a night sufficiently frozen for the bacteria now gathered upon me to be sterilized, though of course I slap globs of sanitizer all about my person regardless of the air temperature. This is a sensible precaution regardless of a restaurant staff's apparent skin health. Dottie's skill with the tennis racket spared her from isolation at the Pickard School, however, and her robust form from an excess of mockery, and I suppose others are less offended by freckles than I.

As much as she loved her uncle, and as much as she shared his appetite for belief, Dottie abandoned the illiberal church over its opposition to women's suffrage. After marrying her first husband, Ar-

To Annie

He who clothes the lilies
And marks the sparrows fall
Protect and save you Annie
And keep you safe thro' all

Your Schoolmate

Lettie Rhodes

Jan 14, 1888.

nold Horn, the portraitist, she fell into theosophical circles, mostly out of her fondness for Eastern dress and decor; but they provided an undemanding fellowship. She wrote a song cycle for piano and voice that chronicled the rise and fall of the empire of Mu—a sunken continent of the Pacific, whose ethereal, enlightened inhabitants still have much to teach us, despite their being drowned—printed and appreciated in several relevant newsletters. Dottie's second marriage—Mr. Horn drank carbolic acid under puzzling circumstances—was to John William Cole, a Blatavsky protege. In Cole's Central Park West penthouse, Dottie adopted the name "Artemis" and acquired, between all the séances and orgies, a world-class collection of Chinese dressing screens.

She is interred in Calvary Cemetery, Queens, or so says the literature. I couldn't find her grave. I did enjoy a passable gyro from the halal truck parked at the cemetery gate—well worth the $3.50, hungry mourners.

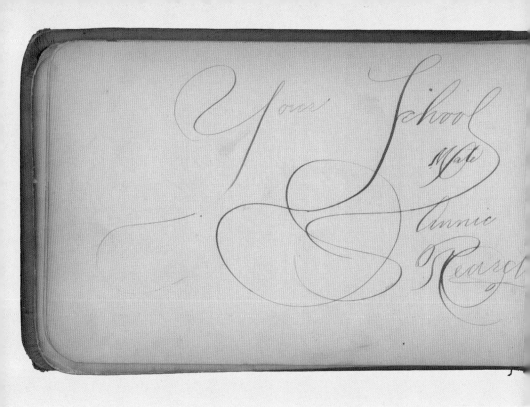

Such delusional grandiosity afflicts the handwriting of Annie Reardon, a younger sibling of Katie, who enjoyed her own earlier note. This is a product of self-hatred: the more florid the surface, the deeper runs the rot. My signature is a blur in which only the *T* and *D* are readily identifiable. The interior of the *D*, the curved section of which is substantial, encloses my subsequent letters, save for the long, rapid tail of my *s*. I expect this means something, although I don't know, and don't want to know, just what.

Annie R. was less corpulent but lots uglier than her sister. Her nose had been broken in early girlhood and improperly repaired, if repaired at all; it resembled, in time, a pelican's beak warped by an unfortunate confrontation with a boat motor, and was prone to congestion and bleeding. She sported a weak chin embedded in a double fold. A permanent downward curve to her lips; even her smile resembled nothing nicer than the grimace of a constipated person riding out a gastric jolt. Strands of hair you could crack like kindling, if you could gather enough to form a strand. And there's nothing worse than wispy eyebrows: how corpselike these make a face. I feel bad. I do.

Somehow, Annie R. married—it's remarkable, I think, how many people did, but desperation prods one into extreme action, and re-

Your School
Mate
Annie
Reardon

pression, meanwhile, yields an equality of result. It was a kind of sexual socialism. Though alas the dreary socialism of bread lines, concrete tower blocks, penal colonies, Stasi surveillance, machine gunners wearing long coats and fur hats, ravening guard dogs, and so on. I'd support the socialism of campfire sing-alongs and lunar colonies and not being obliged to suffer demeaning employment. Such seems unlikely to be achieved, alas, until the invention of compelling androids—decades away, the relevant journals tell me. In any event, Annie and her husband, a Bart Buckley, raised a family and lived a life; they were, perhaps, even content, for which I would applaud them, were it proven true.

In after years when this you see
I wonder what your name will be

your Friend
Kittie J. Sterling
Vanceboro
Maine

School days

Katherine Jane Sterling, of the West Virginia coal Sterlings, married Silas Jackson Oglethorpe, a Georgia railroad scion, whom she met at the races at Charleston Downs, where his horse competed. He owned Oglethorpe Mountain, a neo-Gothic monstrosity overlooking the Chattahoochee River, and the acres of overabundant wilderness surrounding it. Oglethorpe, with his villain's slicked hair and twisted mustache and twirling cane, presented a sinister figure. He was a destroyer of fortunes, a kicker of dogs, a philanderer, a wife-beater, a dedicated anti-Papist, a card cheat, a Klansman, and a dull and selfish conversationalist. It was of little surprise when his well-perforated corpse, a butcher knife still projecting from its stomach, was found on the floor of his study.

Katherine—she sat calmly by the corpse when the doctor arrived, smoking a Murad in an ivory holder, her dress well stained by her husband's blood—was arrested and charged with capital murder, to the embarrassment of all whose involvement was required. The apologies were perpetual. Her private cell at the county courthouse was appointed with gauze privacy drapes and a Chippendale commode from the mayor's own guesthouse. Mr. and Mrs. Sterling provided daily hot lunches—cooked by their personal chef, a Breton who'd trained under Escoffier at the Paris Ritz—to the jury, who could hardly be expected to reason properly when forced to subsist on the meager fare of the courthouse canteen. Judge Scruggs wore a new sable coat to the proceedings and treated the defendant with avuncular deference. Around town one saw a surprising number of new Mercer Raceabouts, engines shrieking, brass fittings all ashine.

The verdict was, of course, not guilty. In due time Buck Simmons, an itinerant laborer of Muscogee County, was apprehended, tried, and convicted, and sentenced to hang, which he did, all in the space of three months, a triumph of law. Katherine assumed her inheritance and returned to Oglethorpe Mountain, where she invested in flocks of peafowl and Greco-Roman statuary by the crateload. Her legendary gardens may still be viewed for a modest admission fee. The autumn sunset, as viewed from the solarium on the south lawn, remains stunning.

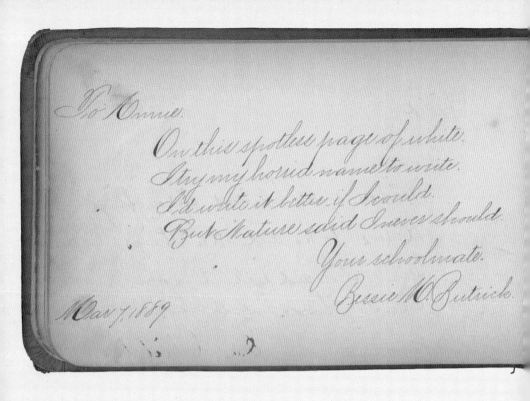

To Annie.

On this spotless page of white.
Stay my horrid name to write.
I'd write it better if I could.
But Nature said I never should.

Your schoolmate.
Bessie M. Butrick.

Mar 7, 1889

"Bessie Butrick" is a horrible name indeed. I'd feel sorry for its owner were I not so soaked with disgust. It rolls off the tongue as sweetly as a spoonful of shit would roll in. She could be the most beautiful woman on the planet—the sort for whom, under normal circumstances, bull-necked princes would scale towers and disembowel witches, kings would assemble war fleets to rescue, billionaires would ruin themselves decking in furs and entertaining in penthouses and tropical resorts—and it would not matter. My bloodless groin is as icy and still as a Klondike morning. The hairs of my mustache remain in place, unraised, their grooming immaculate. "Bessie Butrick." You can smell a horse stall when you say it aloud.

Apparently she was a dear, though, and apparently others are not so affected as I by hideous words. Bessie married John Galvin, a pharmacist from Worcester, and bore eight children in Elm Park, a leafy district of that city, which is today, so far as I can tell, uniformly terrifying. During my brief visit—I did not exit my car—I was cursed at by a clot of red-faced boys outside a windowless tavern, all wearing sweatshirts and chain-smoking, one of whom hurled at my rear window a ball of gravel and ice; and I viewed a poignant, frowning street-walker, her hairy forearms amply bruised, her teeth uneven, her flabby

To Annie.

On this spotless page of white.
I try my horrid name to write.
I'd write it better if I could.
But Nature said I never should.

Your schoolmate.
Bessie M. Butrick.

Mar 7, 1889

---

white buttock oozing like cake batter from an ill-sealed springform pan through a tear in her stockings, which had been purchased, I expect, for a younger, more slender self.

Bessie's son Edward Galvin served three nonconsecutive terms in the Massachusetts House of Representatives and unsuccessfully contested several Senate primaries. Her grandson Jacob Galvin wrote a praised, though mercifully little sold, roman à clef about a privileged boy coming of age in a New England town mauled by postindustrialism. I read several pages while browsing in a Barnes & Noble, waiting for my reservation at a nearby bistro, and was moved to take all six copies from their shelf and hide them in the Art section, behind an album of bichons frises dressed in funny costumes. Appreciate my effort, reader, for it made me late for my supper, and, though seated, I was neglected by my waiter and overcharged for my corked wine.

To my friend

When your husband at you flings
Knives, forks and other things
Seek relief and seek it soon
In the handle of the broom

Dan Chisholm

Son of John, brother of Wanda ("W. D."). Lanky—he was required to take the role of Lincoln in so many school plays—and pigeon-toed, long-armed yet tiny-handed, with eyes that always seemed on the verge of weeping or seeping, thin purple lips like a bachelor school-master's, and a propensity for allergies in his sinuses, Dan was no one's idea of a matinee idol, or whatever was the equivalent term in eras prior to the advent of popular film. Annie possessed a certain affection for him, it's true, but it was sisterly in nature—they'd known each other since they were children, after all, and he was so unmanly in disposition that she felt compelled to ensure that he was passably foddered (he responded best to gingerbread and milk), and that he'd wiped his face and brushed the crumbs and dog fur from his pants and flattened his hair and remembered his coat before he went out of doors. Dan interpreted these gestures as romantic and resolved to marry Annie, who he had convinced himself, after a time, in the blind-ness of his desperation, was the world's prettiest girl.

At eighteen, established in business as an assistant to his father, who by then was directing a corps of independent salesmen, with a decent income and a secure sum on deposit at the Provident Institu-tion, he purchased an absurd diamond at Vandermeer's of Milk Street,

mounted to a ring of eighteen-carat white gold. The proposal went
poorly. Dan perched on the edge of the settee, rocking, clearing mucus from his throat, passing the ring from palm to palm. Annie, dis-
playing the stoic rejection of reality that would become her hallmark,
and a key element in her style of child-rearing, sat rigid and upright,
never speaking, her lips pursed as if she sucked a penny, her unbroken stare directed at a carved pineapple in the molding. A blushing
Mother McFarlane went to boil a kettle for tea and never returned.
Andrew McFarlane had to pull his mustache over his mouth and bar
his chest with his forearms to disguise his heaves of laughter. Dan's
mien was so abject on the trolley ride home that the conductor allowed him to ride for free. He resold the diamond to Mr. Vandermeer
at a 25 percent loss, sparking a hatred of Dutchmen he carried with
him until his death.

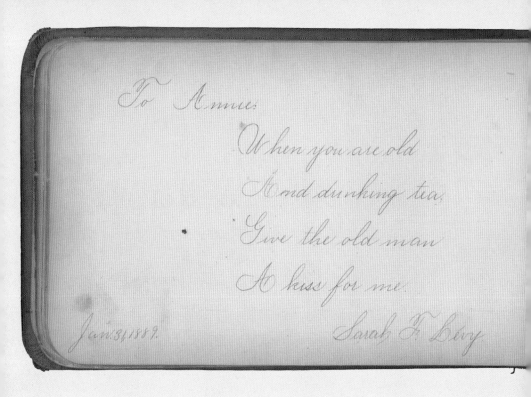

To Annie:

When you are old
And drinking tea,
Give the old man
A kiss for me.

Jan. 3, 1889.   Sarah F. Levy

Annie was sixty-three when Charles Dawes died, an age that I suppose qualifies as "old," particularly at the time of his passing in the 1930s, or when envisioned by teenagers living on the cusp of the Mauve Decade. It seems not so old to me, as I churn into my forties, though I am aging—how undefined the angles of my face have become, how soft my middle, how compromised my eyesight, how tender my spine. And the torpor—such exhaustion crawls upon a person. There are days when I can't be bothered to take calls, change channels, part drapes, or dine. I don't leave my bed at all save to attend the necessary performances in the bathroom.

Annie disliked tea—her preferred invigorating beverages were coffee with breakfast, and coffee with a cordial after lunch. And she would not have kissed poor Charles with such casual affection. I doubt she ever kissed him past the first days of their marriage, when the novelty of Annie's new duties overwhelmed the watchtowers and crossed pikes of her spirit. As I've mentioned—I must have mentioned it—her performance in the marital bed is difficult for me to imagine. We have biological evidence that something happened, to successful conclusion, at least once—with further happenings implied by the low odds

To Annie:

When you are old
And drinking tea,
Give the old man
A kiss for me.

Sarah F. Lévy

Jan. 31, 1889

---

of a single incident of coupling resulting in pregnancy, odds lowered yet further by the famous poor fertility of Dawes males.

There would be no "old man" for Sarah herself, who died four months after applying this note and signature, of the measles, which she contracted while volunteering in a care home for indigents. Her gravestone, at Mount Hope, Boston, is a tapered pillar of violet-scaled marble with a sphere mounted on its pinnacle. Inscribed upon at its base is the motto "Take my yoke upon you and learn from me, for I am gentle and humble in heart, and you will find rest for your souls," which I believe is from the letters of Shelley, tasteful Sarah's favorite poet. The cemetery is a favored place for street people to inject heroin.

Friends are like diamonds.
Few but precious.
Take them like leaves of the
Forest, without number.

Mary E. Bryan
Boston
Mass.

Jan 17th 1889

Were diamonds as abundant in number, and as easy to access, as leaves on trees, they would lose all value. Presently they must be obtained from obscure hemispheres, in volcanic fissures—drawn from miles beneath the surface of the earth by stripped, sweating laborers, artists of the chisel at constant risk of heatstroke, suffocation, and poisoning by fumes. And there's the predilection of ladies—sorry, darlings—for decking themselves in overpriced metals and precious stones, which I assume is a habit driven by innate neurochemistry, given its pronounced character as they achieve a *certain age*, or become the paramours of *certain men*; the preeminence of the diamond in this prevents a rational market from forming, with appropriate prices, and encourages hoarding. And *then* there's the pernicious Boer, who rolls into one queer package—a poorly-wrapped package, with loose flaps, bulging sides, illegible labels, masking tape everywhere, and, inside, rattling, a jumble of damaged, disassembled goods—most of your favorite Semitic and Appalachian stereotypes. It baffles that these flabby, greedy, violent, inarticulate, degenerate hicks were allowed to corner a market, managed to corner a market, a lucrative market, when one can't even conceive of them managing a corner market without resorting to slave labor and tax fraud.

Friends are like diamonds;
Few but precious;
Take them like leaves of the
Forest, without number.

Mary E Bryan
Boston
Mass.

Jan 17th 1889

Mary Bryan attended Mount Holyoke after high school, majoring in English literature—she loved Webster and Landor—and dropping out after her junior year to wed William Armour Pringle, a glaring-bald but otherwise attractive academic. Pringle's biography of John Lilburne, *The Lily Among the Thorns*, is unreadable today—its style is a labyrinth of archaisms, its content unduly speculative—but was regarded as a triumph at the time of its publication. He later taught at Dartmouth, where Mary kept for him a handsome gabled house and baroque garden, birthed at least three children, and styled daily, before a giltwood Regency mirror, her abundant coils of ash-colored hair. Mary's great-great-grandson Derek Gagnon is serving an eight-year prison sentence for robbing, while armed with an unlicensed Sig Sauer 9mm pistol, a few hundred opioid pills from the pharmacy at a Seabrook, New Hampshire, CVS. His knuckles are tattooed.

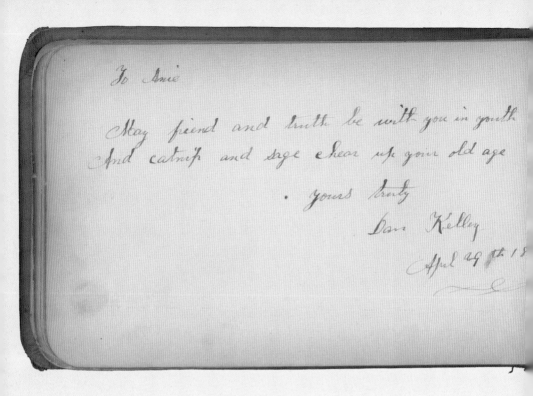

To Annie

May friend and truth be with you in youth
And catnip and sage cheer up your old age

· Yours truly

Dan Kelley

April 29 th 18

Danny Kelley was a neighborhood boy—a touch slow of mind, but courteous, and from a family that kept a clean house. His sole ambition was to play baseball, and he was paid to do so for several years, however meager his achievements. Such tepid accomplishment ought still be savored, I guess. Danny played in Rochester, Hartford, Providence, Buffalo, Keokuk, et cetera: such was the itinerant lot of the reliable but unexceptional ballplayer. In 1901, while with the Savage Reds of Utica, his unattended cigar torched the visitor's dugout at the Mohawk Palace, sparking a lawsuit—sparking!—that set new precedents for employee liability in New York State. He lost his maxillary right central incisor in a fistfight with "Crab" Burkett, of the St. Louis Browns, whom he accosted while drunk outside a Long Island oyster house, Christmas week, 1903. We should remember that baseball, back then, was not the sport of glib, athletic millionaires, but rather of unwholesome, unbathed, beetle-browed slobs to whom book-learning and authentic labor were laughable anathema—men who might nowadays aspire to play poker on television.

However good-hearted, Danny acquired from his teammates the usual unsavory habits of the bottle and of the flesh. He left all across the East wrecked hotel rooms and unsatisfied creditors; and he ruined

[25v]

To Anie

May friend and truth be with you in youth
And catnip and sage chear up your old age

yours truly
Dan Kelley

April 29th 188

an Iowa dairyman's daughter, who died while delivering a stillborn boy, and a seamstress from Geneseo, whose unacknowledged son with Danny was killed at Château-Thierry.

Danny's last appearance in the historical record—that I cared, anyway, to locate—comes on page three of the March 14, 1906, Hot Springs *Courier-Picayune*. A column recounts, in peculiarly heightened language, his rescue of a stray girl from the path of an out-of-control carriage. His dress is compared to "a strutting peacock's, were peacocks prone to crawling up chimney flues," and his mustache is described as "after the fashion of good King Wilhelm, to whom Mr. Kelley claims, if asked, a distant cousinship." We should assume that, on some near subsequent date, Danny returned to a floral, humid rented room, drank whiskey all evening in his underclothes, and died aspirating on his own sick—as one does.

Carrie Sprague.
Vanceboro.
Maine.

Mar. 6—1888.

The twin Sprague sisters, Carrie and May, were classmates of Annie's
at the Vanceboro School—local girls on scholarships, the daughters of
Lester Sprague, who owned the general store.

"Sprague" is my mother's maiden name, though I don't believe
there's any relation. I haven't an immediate means, or an adequate
store of patience, to find out. Mother and I have not spoken for several months. As far as I know, she remains in the American Southwest,
migrating between Taos, where she owns a gallery, and Sedona; it was
in Sedona that I last saw her, visiting Thanksgiving week. Wednesday evening I was subjected to a "Thanks, Genocide" party at which a
plump dwarf in a serape lectured us on the subject of reparations, and
at which no alcoholic beverages were available. On the holiday itself
I was served a meal of Anasazi beans, steamed squash, and millet,
above which I was compelled to swirl, before tucking in, a selenite
crystal suspended from a holy cord. My fellow guests, flanking me at
the long, unfinished ironwood table, included August Rama, a gaunt
Tantric guru in a mandarin collar who smelled of incense burned in a
fromagerie, and Rona X., a sculptress who made a line of ceramics—
ashtrays, chip-and-dips—shaped like vulvas, popular with tourists in
the local tchotchke shops. Our conversations were brief, tense. And

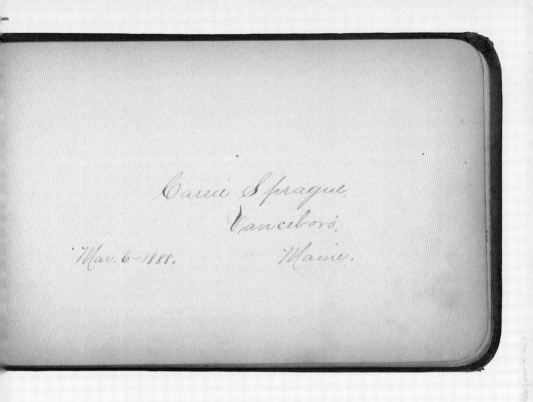

Carrie Sprague
Vanceboro,
Mar. 6—1888.   Maine.

over the weekend, I was expected to feign indifference to the compulsive nudity of Mother and her friends as they splashed about in the Jacuzzi and heated lap pool. My generosity of spirit has boundaries, all starkly delineated when mapped, and in person guarded by razor wire and machine-gun nests. I drank my drinks, paced my room, and on Sunday summoned a livery driver in the morning dark.

I've not had contact with my Sprague uncles and cousins, numbers prolific, since Mother fled, in my youth, to her drier, less tethered climes. They're concentrated, I believe, in central Massachusetts, with their highest density at Leominster. A cadet branch, founded by prodigal Uncle Pete, is spread across upstate New York. Picture, if you will, residential trailers insulated with duct tape, gardens fertilized with the motors of old washing machines, blood-black fingernails, recurrent prosecutions for disability fraud and the decapitation of parking meters. What a fun bunch.

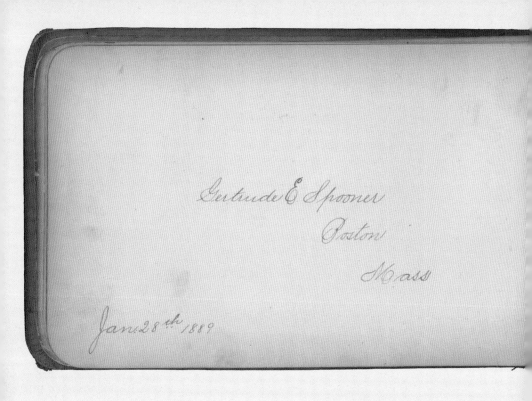

In 1906, Gertie Spooner, already an old maid, struck up a correspondence with a gentleman, a salesman called MacAllister, whom she had met over a plate of liver and bacon at her favorite luncheonette. MacAllister's script was a meticulous thrill, his manners and prose exquisite; such attention flattered immensely, given Gertie's appalling plainness and her lack of interests beyond embroidery, at which she was not skilled, and dime romances, which she had trouble distinguishing from reality. Against the advice of her sister, Mildred, in whose household she resided, and her friends, of which she had a surprising several, she accepted his invitation. On a June afternoon, hauling a carpetbag and parasol, Gertie boarded a train at South Station, Boston, bound for Springfield, Albany, and points west, disembarking the next morning at Cleveland, where she purchased a carnation from a tragic-looking flower girl, drank a hot tea in the commissary, dispatched a postcard to her sister, and purchased a ticket for the 11:15 B&O to Canton. She was not seen again.

MacAllister insisted that she never arrived, and it could not be proven otherwise. I will provide no resolution, I'm afraid. Grounds for official investigation were scant, particularly by the standards of the era, when a person remained free to vanish. Mildred considered

[26v]

Gertrude E. Spooner
Boston
Mass

Jan. 28th 1889

engaging a Pinkerton, but it would just have been too spendy; there were four children who needed feeding, and her husband, sweet in nature but an episodic boozer, was not dependable in his labor. The house felt a sweeter, lighter place with Gertie gone, anyhow. Her hangdog face and irresolute nature had suffused the premises like an anxious vapor, greasy on the skin, smelling of mushrooms and wet socks, clouding the eyes like cataracts. The back bedroom, now spare, provided good space for Mildred's sewing machine, and her piece-work paid her sons' tuitions at Saint Ignatius Day School in Brookline. Francis X., the eldest, enjoyed a long executive career in ice cream manufacture, and is responsible for the promulgation of the Creemee Cup, that childhood favorite in which milk-flavored ice crystals are eaten from a wax cone with a blade of splintered plywood. An inter-change on I-95, near Needham, is named for him.

[27r]

"To Annie:—

"May you always be happy,
And live at your ease.
Get a kind husband you can,
Kiss when you pleas.

"Your Sister.
"Mary M. McFarlane.

"Vanceboro. Feb. 17th 1888.

"For-get-me-not.

Two-and-a-half years Annie's junior, little Mary was many things that her sister was not—physically attractive, for instance, and eclectic and vigorous in activity, and engaged with the wider world, and a pleasant person with whom to keep company. A red-haired, bright-eyed wonder. Her mouth always pursed, as if restraining her instinctive smile.

She met her husband, Paul Hyland—the critic, and later editor of *Suffolk Quarterly*—after writing him a long letter, its prose as lithe and musical as Mary herself, challenging his flippant dismissal of Walter Pater in the review pages of the Boston *Weekly Ledger*; Paul, a good lad in spite of his questionable aesthetic instincts, recanted, and came calling with a bundle of roses. Seven children, none of whom died prematurely, all of whom grew up to be spirited and successful gentlemen or well-wed, pretty ladies, and after whose births Mary retained a good figure. Her homes—a Back Bay townhouse; a rambling, friendly monster, Stick style, in West Cambridge; in Paul's retirement, an arc of Art Deco in the Lexington woods—were spectacles of decorative taste and restraint, and might have been the subjects of magazine features, of coffee-table books, had Mary been a person vulgar enough to slit the bleating throat of privacy on the altar of praise and minor

To Annie :—

"May you always be happy;
And live at your ease;
Get a kind husband you can,
Kiss whom you please,"

Your Sister

Mary H. McFarland

Vanceboro Feb 17th 1858

notoriety. Annie sent a bouquet to Mary's wake, but refused to attend; a rift over the division of their father's estate was never mended.

Mary: a delight, Mary, I think. There is, I believe, enough genetic distance for me to express how alluring I find her photos without blundering into incestuous territory. A reunion with eligible bachelorettes of the line should, perhaps, be organized. My blood relation to her children's children's children's children must be so dilute that, were one of them and I to breed, the chance of our producing a monstrosity would be quite small. It seems a sensible choice, were I to subject myself once more to domestication. This is how Europe constructed its ruling aristocracy. That aristocracy included many alluring ladies, and many handsome men with precise hairstyles and gorgeous suits of evening clothes.

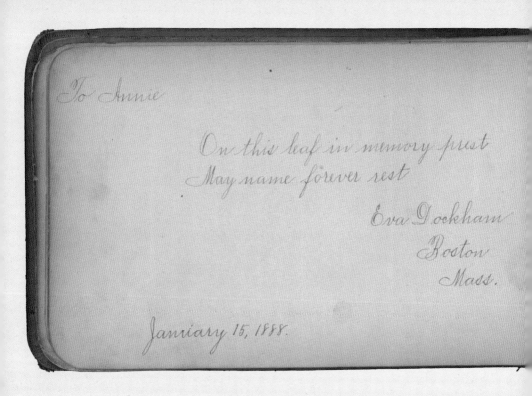

To Annie

On this leaf in memory prest
May name forever rest

Eva Dockham
Boston
Mass.

January 15, 1888.

The Dockhams lived down the street from the McFarlanes in Boston—the nicer end of the street. Their house, behind its hedges and ivies, loomed like a cathedral above its neighbors, and Mr. Dockham—Edward—had ensured that it was equipped with the same world-class plumbing he enjoyed in New York, where he executed his occasional duties for Standard Oil. How one loved the force of the rapid faucets, and the chesty, catarrhal rumble of the flushed toilets. Above the fireplace in Mr. Dockham's study—into which older children were welcome to enter at will, provided that any books they borrowed or objects they disturbed (lion statuettes, Swiss pens, sheets of flecked cream-colored writing paper, the carved scale model of the Parthenon) were returned to their appointed places—hung an oil portrait of Edward Dockham Sr. by Sargent. A highlight of every tour, the painting is now in the collection of the Museum of Fine Arts, though not on display; like most of Sargent's work, it isn't actually that good. Still, the Dockhams and their children participated in all the neighborhood affairs. They attended parties, brought roasts and cakes to the ill, shared church pews, gossiped, and golfed, just as if they weren't so flagrantly everyone's superiors.

To Annie

On this leaf in memory prest
May name forever rest

Eva Dockham
Boston
Mass.

January 15, 1888.

Annie and Eva played often when young, enacting with their dolls an elaborate fantasy in which they were widowed mothers forced by calamity into sharing a tenement apartment. Landlords were always raising the rent, and had not the slightest sympathy for their plight. Constables were always about, soliciting bribes, threatening work-houses and orphanages. The girls shivered with cold, shuddered with starvation, and most often their little dolls died.

Eva married Ernest Lyle Lodge, a Washington attorney and tan-gential relation of the famous political Lodges. Their splendid town house was the subject of a *Ladies' Home Journal* feature. Their son, John Edward Lodge, was, for a time, the record holder for swiftest solo sail across the Indian Ocean, fourteen days from Perth to Zanzi-bar, where he held an appointment in the American consulate.

[28r]

To Miss. Annie McFarlane
Jan. 1. 1888.

When you are far away
And other friends you see
Think of the friends you met in Boston
And among them think of me

John Chisholm

Son of Peter Chisholm, a horse doctor in Methuen, and Sarah Davies, a seamstress of untraceable background. Father of Dan (24r, 28v) and Wanda (9v). Husband to Eleanor Wapping Chisholm, whose great-grandfather, Major Chadwick Wapping, was a hero of the Battle of Saratoga—a jewel of a heritage, this, though of course no one cares about such things, nowadays, aside from bored historians and sufferers of peculiar species of autism; nevertheless, a bronze statue of the major was raised, and remains standing, upon the town common of the Wapping family's native Greenbury, New Hampshire. Occasional colleague, occasional competitor, frequent companion of Andrew McFarlane's. Shaped like a pigeon or a bowling pin, depending on the cut of his coat.

Mr. Chisholm was the sort of person whom, upon meeting, you wished to get to know, and whom, upon getting to know, you wished to get away from. He bantered and laughed and winningly grinned; he grasped one's forearm and squeezed one's shoulder in his warm, familiar way; he ensured that one's punch glass continuously brimmed, and that one ate one's fill of angels on horseback and watercress sandwiches; he inquired after the well-being of one's children, remembering their names and ages and schools. All this was a ruse to

To Miss. Annie M. ... Garlan...
Jan. 1. 1888...

When you are far away
And other friends you see
Think of the friends you met in Boston
And among them think of me

John ...

determine the degree of one's interest in the wholesale purchase of textiles. If one's degree of interest was low—typically the case outside of his offices—then it was to determine the degree of one's tolerance for lectures on philately, Mr. Chisholm's preferred recreation. Mr. Chisholm's breath went thick and foul and his voice took on an aspect of reverential ardor, as if he spoke of an inaccessible lover. One ceased to be asked questions, and no space for questioning—let alone a shift in subject—was provided. A second brandy after dinner would bring the stamp book from its glass case. One would be suffered to leave at midnight, having just missed the last train home, and be forced to walk four miles, in frozen December, through mud-gutter slums.

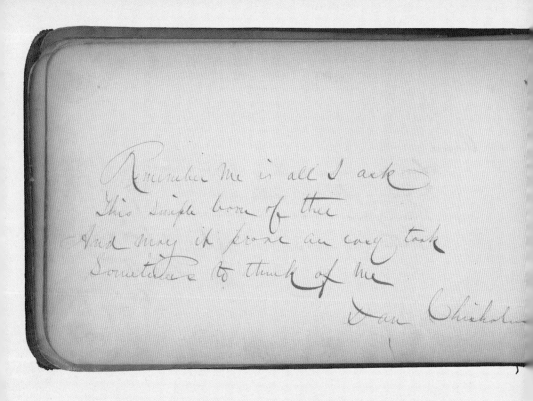

Remember me is all I ask
This simple boon of thee
And may it prove an easy task
Sometimes to think of me

Dan Chisholm

In spring 1898, after Messrs. Hearst and McKinley, at the behest of their cabal of red-nosed, multiply chinned industrialists, conspired to detonate the *Maine*, dear Dan, in a fit of patriotic fury he soon regretted, joined the Navy. The atmosphere on bases and below decks— drenched in the era's repression, electrified by the era's masculine vigor—was foul-mouthed, sexually degenerate, and revolting in odor. While steaming for the Philippines, Dan's ship, the USS *Monadnock*, an armored gunboat, was caught in an out-of-season cyclone, in the vicinity of the Marquesas Islands; the ship survived intact, but Dan was thrown overboard, or jumped. He spent a two nights and a day adrift, per his debriefing, sustained by the splintered slat of a cargo crate, before washing up on an atoll's pearlescent fringe. Here he made the best of things—a hut of palm fronds, experiments with tropical fruits, primitive toolmaking, gnawed nuts, and half-remembered Scout lessons in fire-starting. At some point he was joined by a blue macaw, to which he taught the alphabet and the Lord's Prayer.

Months on—time becomes, you know, an uncertain blur—another storm struck, and its winds raised from the sea a new sandbar connecting Dan's island to a verdant neighbor. As Dan cautiously crossed, a nude, well-tanned man emerged from the brush ahead, hollering in

Remember me is all I ask
This simple boon of thee
And may it prove an easy task
Sometimes to think of me

Dan Chisholm

Spanish, arms raised and waving, his black beard broken by a yellow grin. This was Commodore Garcia Loaiza y Gongora of Cadiz, who, perhaps wrecked in the very same cyclone as Dan, had been living a parallel existence—although *his* palm constructions were weather-tight, and displayed a pleasing Moorish aspect about their arches and joints. Dan heroically beat Loaiza to death with a piece of driftwood, avenging Cuba and proving his manhood in a single stroke, or several dozens of strokes, actually. He took up residence on Loaiza's now-vacant island, enjoying its excellent shelter, efficient rain-collection systems, and tuber crops. In August 1900 a passing transport ship sighted Dan's bonfire; returned to Manila, he was promoted to petty officer second class, awarded three frilly chest medals, and attached to the governor-general's office as a clerk. In 1907, following a shrug of a court martial, he was hanged as a pederast at Subic Bay. He was *very* guilty. My gracious.

[29r]

Annie

When you are sailing down the river of life
In your little bark canoe
May you have a pleasant trip
With only room enough for two,

Brother
Charlie

Elder brother Charles McFarlane—freckled, button-nosed, auburn-haired, long-legged, astigmatic Charlie—was eight years Annie's senior. He took after his mother, both physically—long limbs, narrow torso, doll's feet—and in his soft temperament. His father treated him like a pet bird, bestowing on him habitual utterances and handfuls of seed and patting his extravagant crest, but locking him in a quiet back room, in a tarp-covered cage, when respectable guests arrived—so wrote Mary McFarlane in her wonderful diary.

Charlie dropped out of Boston College a year short of graduating, claiming to his indulgent parents an exhaustion of the spirit. He spent months holed up in his room, subsisting on water and milk crackers, reading his Bible and a volume of Milton, recording in miniature script sheet after sheet of private notes that he scrambled to cover with his pillows and quilts if anyone violated his threshold. When he emerged, unshorn and fragrant, with spidery hairs projecting from his nape, Charlie announced that he had uncovered a truth of the greatest profundity, the unknown artery that pulsed behind the skin of things.

"I must go to the diocese," he insisted, a sheaf of yellow paper under his arm, a glaze of sweat on his ashen brow. Annie prevailed upon him to change from his crimson long johns into an outfit less impious.

Annie

When you are sailing down the river of life
In your little bark canoe
May you have a pleasant trip
with only room enough for two ?

Brother
Charlie

That evening a messenger boy came bearing a note from the arch-bishop's secretary, assuring the McFarlanes that all was well, and that Charlie was in caring, velvet-gloved hands. Andrew tipped the lad a quarter and ruffled his sandy hair, and Mother McFarlane fed him a ham sandwich.

Charlie returned three weeks later, skinnier than ever, paler than ever, with a patch of white shaped like an aleph in his beard. "I was mistaken," is all he would say of his experience. He accepted a job in the billing department of the Grand Northern Timber Corporation of Vermont, moving to Burlington. Drowned two summers later while swimming in Lake Champlain. His rooms, in an old carriage house near the university, were found to contain only a straw mattress beneath a blanket of raw wool, a bowler hat with a foot-crushed crown, an enamel basin, eighteen dollars in silver coins, and a charcoal sketch of a browsing rabbit.

The Roses red and voileto
blue Shugar is Swet and
So are you

Jennie Day June 1888

A Vanceboro local, Jennie Day was the daughter of Maurice Day, a signalman on the Maine Central, and Jill Leblanc, a native of Quebec. Gifted with a fine voice, Jennie could often be heard singing traditional French-Canadian songs—set to morose melodies, tales of Indian guides and their birchbark canoes, sexually frustrated monks, lonely loggers, and bears and moose all afrolic—accompanied by her mother, a deft hand with parlor instruments. Her voice slid through the stillness of the rural night like a scalpel through soft tissue. Andrew McFarlane covered his head with his pillow and stuffed his ears with cotton and cursed all morning over his coffees, but Annie was enchanted, and sat in her nightdress with her elbows propped on the windowsill, her chin resting on her palms. *"Qu'apporte-tu dans ton jupon? C'est un paté de trois pigeons."* Mrs. Day attempted to teach a curious Annie some chords on the guitar and piano, and Jennie to coach her on how to smoothly sustain sung notes; but Annie had no musical talent, and her aptitude for rote learning was undermined, here, by her stumpy fingers and adenoidal voice. Annie decided that she disliked music, declaring it frivolous as a pastime and impenetrable, and therefore fraudulent, as an art.

The roses red and voilets
Blue Shugar is Sweet and
So are you

Jennie Day

Jan 1888

Jennie did not attend the Vanceboro School—its tuition was not plausible on a railwayman's salary, if she'd have even been admitted. She instead did her learning at the local one-room grammar school (the fruits of this education are evident in her note), and then at the public high school in Houlton, rooming in town there with a spinster cousin. At seventeen, a month short of graduating, she married Andrew McTavish, a classmate who'd just inherited his father's farm, and for him performed the usual—it's wearing on me, how usual it is—housewife and mother routine, all the way until October 1914, when she fell ill after eating bad apples, and died of an unidentified intestinal complaint. Her great-grandson, a fellow called Jason Scarpetto, is a systems analyst who lives in Hopedale, Massachusetts, two municipalities northwest of Uphamshire, the postal village in which I was raised. We've never met.

[30r]

To Annie,

A little word in kindness spoken,
A motion, or a tear,
Has often healed the heart that's broken
And made a friend sincere.

Your Friend,—
Margie E. Frasier

Boston, Jan. 11th,/89

The Frasiers were a fine family: I bestow upon them all my approval—its bottle is overturned above them until the final rivulet has cleared its lip. They inhabited a three-story maisonette on the first, best block of Marlborough Street. Mr. George Frasier, a graduate of Yale, was an independent researcher in ornithology, widely published and respected in the field, and wore the most immaculate beard I've ever seen. A late photograph shows an unbroken sheet of glossy hair descending from his high, hewn cheeks, as soft as angora wool, all agleam in the magnesium flash. He must have been barbered daily—perhaps he even kept a barber on call, on retainer, as perfect a luxury as can be conceived. (I submit to biweekly sessions and am ever dissatisfied by the slapdash, uneven efforts of the tattooed lads and grizzled Turks on whom I hesitantly bestow, and from whom I always, always withdraw, my custom.) Mrs. Meredith Frasier, née Scheufel, claimed some kinship, close enough to raise brows rather than roll eyes, to the king of Bavaria, and was a cousin of a cousin of a Hapsburg. A handsome woman with a bust as immense as the Zugspitze and a great Teutonic nose on which you could have impaled a grapefruit, if such an act appealed to you.

To Annie,

A little word in kindness spoken,
A motion or a tear,
Has often healed the heart that's broken
And made a friend sincere.

Your Friend,
Marge E Frasier

Boston, Jan 11th /89

Margaret Frasier was the Prize Day speaker on her graduation from the Pickard School, and encouraged her fellow young ladies to embrace modern opportunity as only their loving arms could. She was admitted to Radcliffe, where she obtained a BA *summa cum laude* in history, and wrote, as her thesis, a quite impressive monograph on the Commonwealth of England as the fulcrum of modernity that would have been publishable, that would have been published, had her sex been the sturdier of the two. A few months of a Masters curriculum were completed, but Margaret had met Lawrence Lowell Mercer, then a PhD candidate in the English Department at Harvard, at a boathouse tea in July, and by December had married him. She bore two lawyers, an Andover dean, and a girl who married a Union Carbide vice president. Following an argument over Vico's *Verum factum* principle that escalated to cocktail-tossing, Dr. Mercer exchanged a sequence of insulting letters with Edmund Wilson; these were excluded from Wilson's collected correspondence due to their uncomfortable schoolboy innuendo and scatological content.

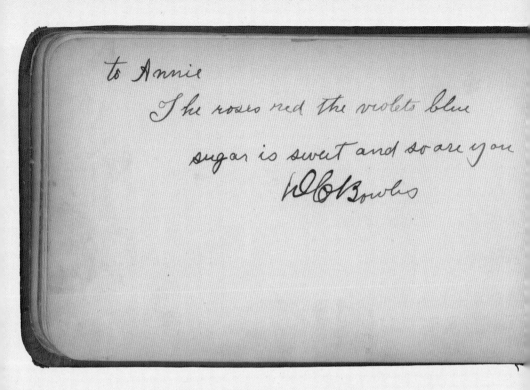

to Annie
The roses red the violets blue
sugar is sweet and so are you
W.D.C. Bowles

See my earlier note.

A trite business, this, and certainly David Bowles had the education to do better. He *does* do a little better, I think, by dropping the typical "are" and adding a "the" from and to the first line—a more urgent, sonorous formulation. But he didn't care, did he? He dashed off a cliché, the most readily at hand of all the ready-made, to fend off an unwanted admirer. Imagine the besotted young—too young— Annie tugging at the hem of David's evening coat, batting at him her brief charmless eyelashes, waving this idiot album. David bared at her his square, wine-stained teeth and provided a tolerant scrawl before stepping into his raccoon overcoat and taking himself outdoors into the alluring snow-blue evening. He was, after all, a Harvard man, and enjoyed better prospects than a glorified salesman's spindly adolescent daughter; and anyway, the indecent services available in low houses and atop alley pallets downtown quenched any urgency he felt around a marriage. Annie, I hope, mooning in her bedroom, read again and again this entry, awareness closing about her like a fog from the sea, the whiff of low tide upon it, as she realized that David could not have given less of a singular shit about her. Perhaps he'd pull her from a pond if she fell through its ice and he happened to be hiking

[30v]

to Annie

The roses red the violets blue
sugar is sweet and so are you

D. G.[?] Bowles

an adjacent trail. Perhaps he'd offer her a shove—or even wrap his hairy, muscular arms about her—were he to observe her in the path of a panicked draft horse. But nothing further: not ever. She need not have cried—the bolts in her spine were ratcheted too tight for tears to freely flow—but it would please me to know that her face turned red as fields of poppies blooming, that she sweated and shivered and knew what a tedious dunce she had made of herself, and how everyone had laughed at her weak, obvious, unreturned ardor.

Charles Dawes was, despite the deep bore of Annie's steel fingernails, a kind and mild man, whose expressions of uxorious sentiment were met with expulsions of the most distilled, cardiotoxic venom.

[31r]

Vanceboro 1888
Febuary 17

Friend. Annie

To knit and spin was once A
Girls employment but now to
Dress and have A beaux is All
A girls enjoyment

From your Friend
S Broderick
Woodstock

Sarah Broderick Woodstock—not to be confused with Sarah Broderick, a silent, mousy girl two grades younger—was another Vanceboro classmate. A daughter of Harold Woodstock, who owned foundries in Buffalo and Tonawanda, Sarah was at little risk of having to resort to work, though her bumpy rhyme points, I suppose, to the anxiety induced by the recurring economic crises and lowborn unrest of the era. The family carriage was often pelted by eggs and vegetable matter when its comings and goings were insufficiently discreet, and on several consecutive May Days members of the American Brotherhood of Molders and Founders tarred and feathered an effigy of Mr. Woodstock, and set it alight in Niagara Square. These rabble were always dispersed by constables, or by Woodstock's squads of Pinkerton bodyguards, but to be ritually murdered on an annual basis sets even the most complacent mind to wonder and worry.

Still, Sarah was appealing in face and figure, and an excellent dresser—though who wouldn't be with her budget?—and had her winning manner; in the most dreadful class of outcomes imaginable she still could have charmed a bookkeeper or a bank clerk, who would have felt himself very lucky indeed, and kept her in a degree of comfort, however unsplendid. As it happened, she married Leonard Davenport, a man of leisure she met while changing trains at Penn Station, Pittsburgh, as she traveled home for Christmas break during her sophomore year at Bryn Mawr. They lived at Cockscomb Hall, a ninety-six-room Georgian revival house on the Hudson near Staatsburg. Sarah loved to take her morning tea in the Grecian Room, where, above the fireplace, hung a frieze, taken from Ephesus, of Actaeon peeping through parted reeds at nubile Artemis, and where the windows overlooked the many stolen marbles of the sculpture gardens. Her grandson, John Leonard Davenport, later a *Weekly Standard* columnist, was the architect, in the seventies, of a scheme to seize the Ghawar Field in Arabia; he got as far as a phone call with Edward Heath, and drinks at the Yale Club in New York with the Soviet consul and a disguised Henry Kissinger (aquamarine contacts, horsehair mustache).

The daughter of Hamish Murray, the owner of a Berlin, New Hampshire, paper mill, and Myrna Kelly. Sadie was privately tutored until her dispatch to the Vanceboro School at age thirteen. Unsocialized, and unused to the austerity of dormitory life, Sadie became the cringing mongrel stray of her class, with ragged hair and fingernails gnawed to the nailbed, speaking the minimum number of syllables decency required, and only in response to direct interrogation. She was thus a perfect friend for Annie—dependent on Annie's interest and desperately tolerant of its waxing and waning, with no choice but to weather Annie's moods, which were as varied uncomfortable as the Laurentian climate. Their correspondence after the McFarlanes returned to Boston maintained the same tenor: Annie hectoring, lecturing, insulting; Sadie apologizing, agreeing.

In May 1890, Sadie fell from the Vanceboro School's chapel bell tower and was killed; this was deemed a prank gone wrong by the discreet headmaster, but come on, Dr. Prescott, come right on. There was mourning in Berlin, where Hamish Murray, a generous employer (survivable wages, Christmas geese, books and sports balls for employees' children), was respected; you couldn't see the casket for all the flowers. In the immediate aftermath there descended a hush about the

Vanceboro School, and a sensation of thin oxygen; but a week later, the girls were back to chatter about husbands and piano rolls, and checking the quad for bloodstains and indentations in its turf. Annie sent an agonized letter to the Murrays on which she dripped water from her basin in imitation of tears.

Hamish Murray passed the paper mill on to his son, Jack, who governed it with the same light hand as his father, and who welcomed the unionization of his workforce, and the benefits and privileges thereby gained, as signs of progress and modernity, as much as he did the replacement of his muley saws with electric motorized band saws, which was dear in price but resulted in excellent gains in efficiency. Jack passed the paper mill on to *his* son, Jack Jr., who stripped and sold off the mill's physical assets, fired its workforce, and sold its good name, still deployed today on a line of mealy newsprint, to the Carolina-Atlantic Corporation. He retired to San Diego at age thirty-nine.

[32r]

Your friend and Schoolmate
May Sprague
Vanceboro.
Maine.

May Sprague—Carrie's twin. Annie, like her cohorts, paid little mind to the Sprague girls. Why bother? Their attendance at the Vanceboro School was a courtesy to Lester Sprague, from whom the masters were obliged to order their ivory combs and collar starch.

May's daughter Belinda married her first cousin, Christopher, Carrie's son. Most of their issue left Vanceboro for regions with more remunerative employment and less consanguineous romantic prospects, but two sons stayed: Barry, who took over his grandfather's store, and John Paul, who worked for the Customs Service until he secured his pension, at which point he set himself up as a subsistence scavenger in the woods. Two of Barry's daughters (Lisabet and Deborah) married two of John Paul's sons (Peter and Don). You can see where this leads, with two—or actually three (Spragues are precocious in that regard)—more generations. The present-day proportion of Spragues in Vanceboro's population is quite out of line with the proportion of Spragues in the general population. Consult the telephone directory. Survey the mailboxes. It's appalling. The Sprague infant mortality rate is triple that of the national average, and more than quintuple that of Cuba and Canada. Kaylee Sprague must sleep in an oxygen tent and vacuum the mucus from her lungs; an implanted breathing de-

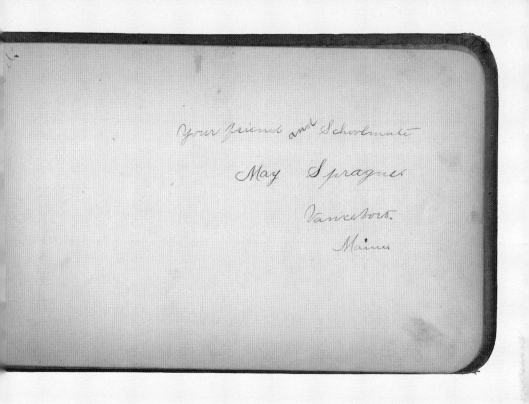

vice in her trachea is in the offing, pending sufficient pledges on the relevant GoFundMe. Bradley Sprague, who has no cuspids, was twice arrested as a teen for attempting sexual congress with his neighbor's mare—a brazen chestnut Morgan called Fran—and is currently awaiting trial for his role in the theft of Coleman fuel, a whole pallet, from the Walmart distribution center in Lewiston. The circumference of Travis Sprague's skull is two standard deviations larger than the average; though blind and only protoverbal, he is a whiz with figures, I must admit. Marco Sprague is a primordial dwarf.

I suffer visions of amber vials and bent syringes cracking underfoot, of crystalline molds, the fragrance of feces, the fragrance of mushrooms, wrists in yellowed casts, eyepatches wrinkled and stained with sweat-salt, swing sets tipped on their sides and overgrown by dry gray grass, mazes and monoliths of PVC piping, diaper pails with missing lids, dead trucks and dead trees, the fury of black flies, the tragic moon.

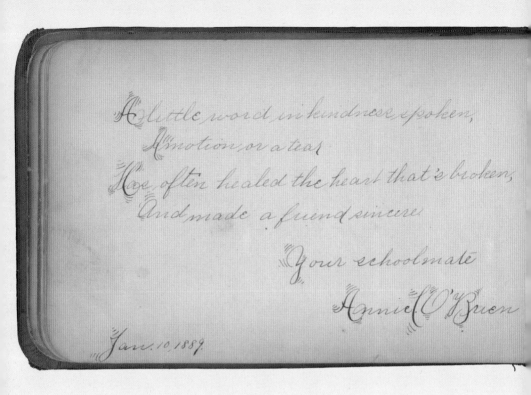

A little word in kindness spoken,
A motion or a tear
Has often healed the heart that's broken,
And made a friend sincere

Your schoolmate

Annie O'Brien

Jan. 10, 1889

These O'Briens were a family whose father, Daniel, an able carpenter, Andrew McFarlane often engaged for home repairs and renovations. A friendship emerged; they liked to drink their drinks together, in the sun room in summer and in Andrew's study in winter, waxing nostalgic about the auld sod upon which neither man ever had or ever would tread, while their wives and children amused themselves in the front rooms.

Annie O'Brien was a bumptious, hoarse-voiced girl, scarlet-haired with freckles in even proportion to unblemished skin, the same age as, and quite disliked by, Annie M., though Annie M. felt compelled to keep this to herself—her siblings and mother found Annie O. an energetic joy. Patiently, patiently, Annie M. would sit on a straight-backed, wicker-seated chair, her hands folded in her lap, as Annie O. read aloud her latest school theme (always graded at 100 percent by her grateful English teacher), played "Für Elise" on the parlor's upright piano at thrice the designated tempo, drew perfect pencil portraits of Mary and Mother McFarlane (Annie M. turned her head and decried the sin of vanity), distributed platters of almond macaroons that she herself had baked that very afternoon, guzzled third servings of tea before anyone else had finished their first, recalled and recited

A little word in kindness spoken,
A motion or a tear
Has often healed the heart that's broken,
And made a friend sincere.

Your schoolmate
Annie O'Brien

Jan. 10, 1889.

---

conversationally relevant passages from the Bible, knew her Shakespeare and her Milton and made sure you knew that she knew; and her wide and overheated lap attracted the affection of Widdershins, the McFarlanes' usually standoffish, indeed violent, eel-slick black cat.

Annie O. was married at eighteen—her enthusiasms could not be contained—to Brian Boyle, a junior clerk for the Boston & Liverpool Line. Annie M. was made to attend the wedding, at which Andrew McFarlane wept elaborately, honking his crushed red nose into a gingham handkerchief, and whistled and clapped and tossed his hat into the air. Annie O. died of sepsis following a difficult childbirth, her third, at age twenty-four. Annie M. was not made to attend the funeral, but did so anyway, smirking discreetly behind her gauzy veil and grinding her sharp heel on her father's foot when he rose to make a speech.

Marcia A Sprague
Vanceboro
Maine

June 8th 1888

Another fucking Sprague. This is Marcia, mother.

The thing I find most galling about *my* mother—Leona Sprague, that is, or Leona Sprague Dawes, or whatever Hindi or Hopi surname she's adopted for the moment—is not the cheap imitation of spirituality, the store-bought mysticism, with which she paints over every occurrence, every action or impulse, interpretation always preceding its object; nor is it her frequent catty remarks, despite being thirty-one years divorced, about my father's arid character, and the rigidity of the steel pole that, she says, sustains the walls of his rectum; nor is it the vulgarity of her recreation, which, despite her advanced age, includes hallucinogenic mushrooms and bisexual orgies—all the withered bodies writhing like dry worms in light breezes—or the click-clack of the oversized costume jewelry with which she decks her ears and neck, the ohm pendants and jade boulders and Jain beads, never knowing what a pretentious monster she appears. No, it's that, despite a relationship with her son that is *clearly strained*, to the point of elastically snapping and blinding, in its recoil, a dozen spectators, and scalding a score more with the gallons of acid that had been therein contained, Mother still behaves as if, Mother still laughably presumes that, she retains a right to pass judgment on the state of my life, and that I care

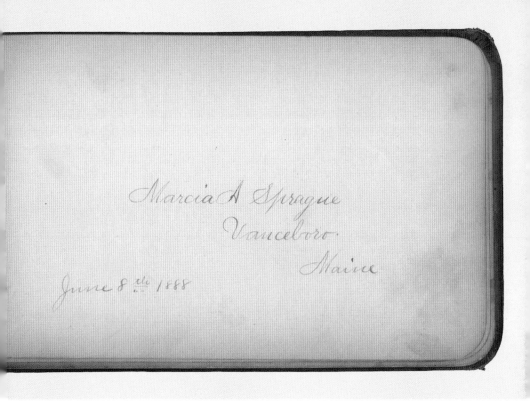

Marcia A Sprague
Vanceboro
Maine

June 8th 1888

for her care. She wonders why this book, why a book at all—she worries, I'm sure, at her portrayal, if any: she's the worst sort of narcissist. She wonders why I don't take on conventional employment, for the security of it, and its steady rhythms—and something with my hands would heal my spirit; she knows a home builder, a bricklayer, if I'm of a mind. I wonder how much money she has tied up in her various properties, her houses and acres. I wonder if it's going to me when she dies, or to another ludicrous fund for illiterate natives or for vapid ruined girls. Years' worth of unpaid, or at least underpaid, taxes would not surprise. I can guess.

"I'm fine," I shout at her. "I'm fine, I'm fine, I'm fine." I end the call and flick my phone onto my bed like rheum from my fingertip. I empty a candy dish full of ashes into the wastebasket.

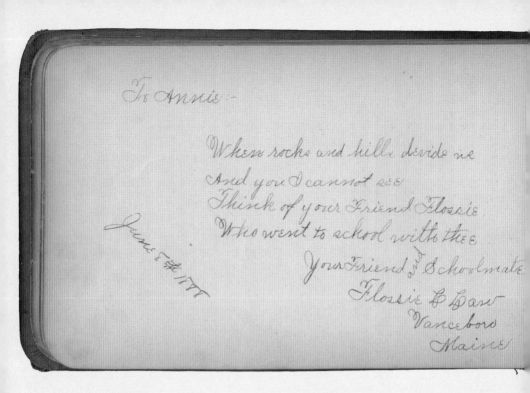

To Annie:—

When rocks and hills divide us
And you I cannot see
Think of your Friend Flossie
Who went to school with thee.

Your Friend & Schoolmate
Flossie B Law
Vanceboro
Maine

June 5th 1888

"Flossie" is the classic name for one's milk cow, and I find it hard to stop picturing Flossie Law as one—a bipedal Holstein, pince-nez perched upon her muzzle, cowbell dangling from her pearl choker, udder discreet behind a frilly apron, which is perhaps decorated with a stitched image of a conventional cow. But of course she was a mere girl, no more exciting than her verse, which is most abjectly not. So far as I can tell, combing through preserved correspondence and photographs, compiling anecdotes from living figures, Annie never mentioned Flossie after leaving Vanceboro, perhaps never gave her a single thought—if Annie enjoyed a tender thought, it would never have been admitted—and this page is the only record of their having known each other.

Flossie's father, Benjamin Law, owned a manufactory of fur hats and coats in Newark, and made smart investments in property all around Upper Manhattan. Her brother Thomas, inheriting all, was a stupidly wealthy man, as were his sons, as are his sons' sons, and I assume their sons, and some daughters, here and there, as well. Scouring the microfiche, one sees many raised highball glasses on the society pages, and long cigars, and white dinner jackets. So many Law Halls in universities all about the northeast, and Law Wings in hospitals.

Envy is beneath a man such as I. Envy is contemptible habit. "I" ought always to be enough. I remind myself—and you, reader—that everyone suffers, everyone dies and rots in the same earth, or is scattered by the same indifferent wind if cremated, which I would prefer not to be, given the exponential advance of technology and the potentialities for revivification inherent therein. Only the Parsis are elevated in death, their corpses being consumed by particular crows and ravens, which are terribly bright birds, with knowable personalities and idiosyncratic preferences; Parsi corpses are, then, incorporated into *real individuals,* and if consciousness does indeed permeate all things down to a subatomic level, who knows what wonderful influence they might exert. Perhaps this is the origin of corvid intelligence.

Flossie married, lived in Rochester and at Seneca Lake, and may well have been consumed by the upstate snow, which is prolific.

To Annie:—

"Let Wisdom be your counselor,
Nor from her guidance cease,
Her way's are way's of pleasantness,
And all her path's are peace.

Your Friend and Schoolmate.
Ethel E. Jameson
Vanceboro.
Maine

June 8th 1888

"Wisdom"—how I hate the word. Its meaning has ceased to be meaningful. When we declare someone or something—a mountain-dwelling ascetic, a motto inscribed on the base of a historic statue—to be wise, what we mean is that we agree with its expressed position. We imply that while we agree, you do not, or are ignorant of the sentiment, and that either of these are the result of inexperience or a flawed character. Wisdom is a tactic, in other words, we deploy to make our own positions inviolable. One needs to know nothing: one needs only to sound convinced. A charismatic corporate founder reminds us of his status as a visionary, featured in magazines, and suggests that forgoing paychecks, for the moment, in exchange for future equity, will bring the Kingdom of Heaven to the earth, with all of Christ's princely angels given seats on the board. Certainly, says the consulting economist, who has after all been in business for years, the sporting arena, which to construct will require extensive land-taking and a 75 percent buy-in from the catastrophically indebted local government, will pay for itself in new revenue, never mind how arbitrary or mysterious its projected sources, never mind the city's crumbling physical plant, the buckling secondary roads, the infrequent buses, the peculiar flavor of the tap water, the layoffs of clerical staff. My mother presses upon

To Annie:–

"Let Wisdom be your counselor;
Nor from her guidance cease;
Her way's are way's of pleasantness,
And all her paths are peace.

Your Friend and Schoolmate.
Ethel E Jamieson
Vanceboro
Maine

June 8th
1888

me some self-published volume with a sans-serif typeface, extra large, and a title like *Moments of Being* or *The Strength of Today*, and a man with a Buddha-bald pate and moist, too-lucid eyes staring from the back cover. Even I am not immune: yonder stalks young Theodore, with his fresh, sparse child's beard and volume of Husserl, stalking across the floor of the Bean Exchange to order the dark triple shot he secretly dislikes, eyebrows cocked above the rims of his spectacles, looking for fellow patrons looking at him, for the first time mistaking, as he will for the rest of his life, his sense of self for relevance in the world.

Argumentum ad verecundiam, these things are called, according to Paul Harshaw, the talented and well-read attorney who represented me in both of my divorces and in all three of my lawsuits (from two of which I emerged with lucrative settlements in hand, but whose amusing details I am, alas, forbidden by terms to disclose), and who has given me excellent advice on my squash grip, and wine cave, and so many other grand topics.

To. Annie

Rember well and bear in mind a trusty friend is hard to find when you find him Just and true never change him for the new years

L McDonald

Sister of Maggie (13r). Daughter of Francine (35r). Niece of Andrew McFarlane. Cousin of Annie. I appreciate Eleanor's sentiment—how nice, how novel, to see fidelity respected and encouraged. Well, not so novel at the time of its expression, but I feel sometimes as if I stand with each foot in a different epoch, the piles of the carpets in each alarmingly disparate.

We obsess, nowadays, not over truth and strength of character and character itself, but over desire. Not only over its fulfillment, but over its absence, too, and the keenness of its blade-edges when found too dull. This is pernicious capitalism—of which rampant consumption is the inescapable result—molding the minds of its subject population. One must raise oneself above it—plug one's ears against its noise, its bullhorns and fireworks. One need not always *want*. One need not always *gain*. I have tried to separate from such modes of thinking in my own life. My needs are so few, now. My wardrobe contains five suits, ten shirts in blue and white, two athletic outfits, two pairs of shoes, a topcoat, and a pair of duck boots for damp weather. I like to live in hotels, to which I'm so much less obliged than an owned home. I rent cars as I need them, and almost always opt for a coupe. I reserve my spending for articles of real value and unique aspect, idiosyncratic luxuries like meals at exquisite restaurants—I betook myself to Napa, for instance, last weekend, to dine at Pralnia, Tomasz Piwinca's bistro, enjoying in particular, among the unceasing felicities of its twelve-course tasting menu, the chaudfroid of sea urchin and the ox heart terrine, and I blinked not once at the bill, of which both the meal and I were worthy—and investments in art and culture, such as my early Freud oil, purchased from a Greenwich widow too slack of wit to hire an appraiser, and my Vallotton woodcuts (presently in secure storage, these), and the cost of material and research and labor for the very text you now read, reader. There's something wholesome, indeed holy, about such restraint, in this unrestrained age. It's as if you've breakfasted on grapefruit and taken a vigorous swim. The belly is tight. The muscles are warm. The flawless skin is scraped of filth.

Everyone else is flabby and ill and has just bathed in a pit latrine.

To Annie,

When this you see
Think of me.

Mrs. John McDonald.
West Acton.
Mass.

The former Francine McFarlane. Mother of Maggie and Eleanor. Sister of Andrew. Aunt to Annie.

Francine enjoyed an easier childhood than did her elder brother. She was doted on, for one, by their father, who daily brought her sweetmeats in wax paper wrappers and who, when it thundered, stroked her hair until she slept. For a second, her presence in the household was an asset rather than a drain—when aged twelve years, the same age at which Andrew was shoved out the front door to find a way in the world, Francine was beating rugs, boiling rounds of beef, scouring pans, darning socks, hemming pants, et cetera, with skill equal to that of a housewife with thirty years' experience. Mother's capacity for taking in laundry was doubled; the store of coin beneath the kitchen's loose floor plank was swiftly doubled, and a summer weekend at Salisbury Beach was countenanced.

Francine didn't care for Annie, finding her sour and pretentious, which I consider a fair assessment: through the weblike strings of genes echo notes of sympathy like struck piano wires. Still, she tried to be kind—Annie was, after all, the merest girl, a pliable one at that, and couldn't help that her father wrapped himself in ermine as soon as he had a few dollars in his pocket, or that her mother was from

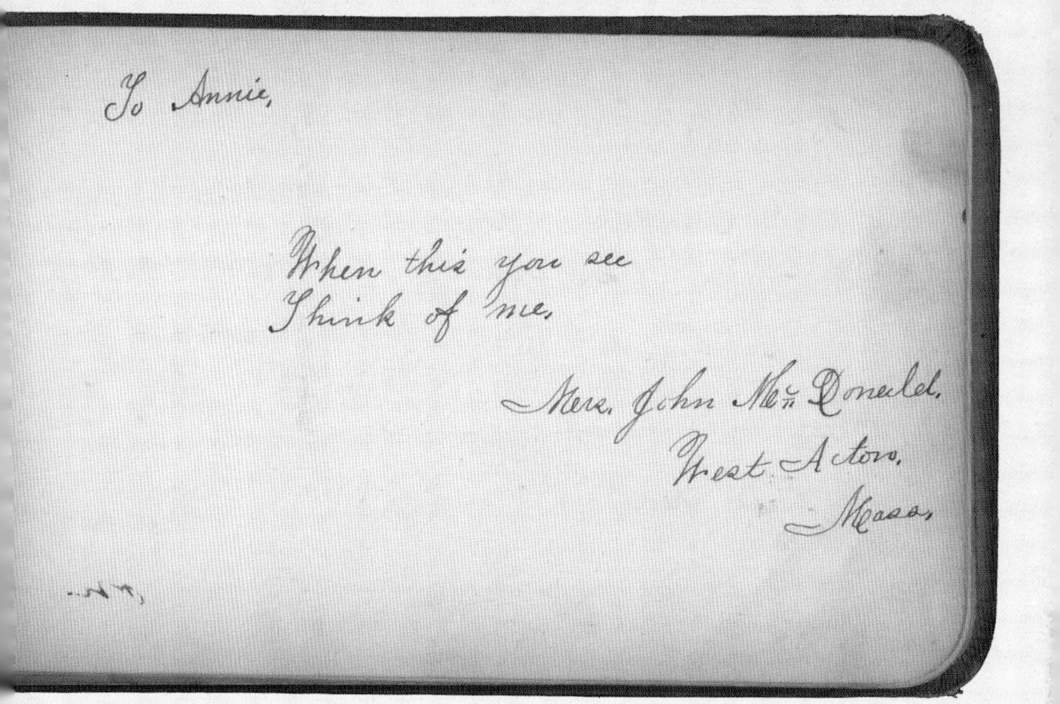

To Annie,

When this you see
Think of me,

Mrs. John Mcᴺ Donald,
West Acton,
Mass,

birth a spoiled prig crowned with a bejeweled circlet. Trips to the Mc-Donald house in Acton, or to the McFarlane house in Boston, were dreaded and resented. Family holidays, family meals, were a cavalcade of passive aggression, and, with drinks—Francine, Andrew, and John McDonald were all prone to intemperance—overt aggression: many glasses were smashed, and dishes shoved onto the floor, and poor Eleanor McDonald was once soaked by a tureen of roast drippings inaccurately tossed.

I ask again to what end a person subjects himself to a family. A misapplied fidelity to tradition is my best guess. That wrongheaded conservatism which seeks to preserve the garden's every briar, rather than to prune and ensure the robust health of its flowers, and the clarity of its views, and its paths, which I think I should like to line with granite stepping-stones, arranged in the Japanese manner.

May your life be always happy
and your smiles be always gay
like the lilies of the Valley When
they bloomin lovely (May)

Miss Lo fro—

Sadie Frank, another school chum, yet another school chum, was the daughter of Hiram Frank, a Saxon burgher who grew his stake in a Jamaica Plain brewery, inherited from a cousin, into the small-scale domination of the production of pilsners throughout eastern New England. This allowed him a lovely large house, with private pond and private woods, at Newton Upper Falls, his own racing horse ("Die Schwarze Rakete") who competed at Suffolk Downs, the excellent hats for which he became known to certain sets of Boston partygoers, hunting trips into remote and exotic climes (overlooking his dining room were the mounted heads of a polar bear, a Malay rhino, a Sudanese king crocodile, an Andean clouded jaguar) and fine educations for his children (the Pickard School and Mount Holyoke for Sadie, Nobles and Harvard for son Herman). Handsome devil, too, with a nutcracker nose and a long mustache that he swept to each side and waxed to needlelike points. I would like to wear such a mustache myself, but the hairs of my face have a difficult texture, and the relatively short distance between my nose and my upper lip—compared to that of a conventional gentleman, that is to say—does not provide sufficient space for growth to occur in compensatory profusion.

Sep 24 188
to Annie B

May your life be always happy
and your smiles be always gay
like the lilies of the valley when
they bloomin lovley May

Miss S Frank

Don't Forget

Sadie married Jacob Breitner, the son of Hiram's officer of finance. They moved, for their own safety, to Havana after the Zimmerman telegram, and, for several years' emotional recuperation, to Cavalaire-sur-Mer on the Riviera. Their cosmopolitan sons became figures of use in the Department of State and the OSS. A grandson married an Astor.

I've never been sure what a lily of the valley actually was, though of course I've read and heard five million references. Having now looked them up, I can say I've seen them five million times. Having now looked them up—oh, boring flowers, deadly boring. I prefer lilacs and bluebells, their calming colors and torpid summer odors; morning glories are nice as well, though their vines, when untended, or tended not as I prefer, take on qualities I find uncomfortable to look at, down to the very pilings of my soul, assuming I've got one.

[36r]

To Annie

Beefsteak when you are hungry
Soda when you are dry
Money when you are hard up
And heaven when you die

your friend and
shoolmate
Ida
Prager

Beefsteak was considered a health food in the nineteenth century. It fortified the blood, energized the loins, and drew the muses to the brain. "Steak pills"—that is, capsules of extract—were sold by druggists to the anemic, the weak-kneed, the hollow-chested; Capt. Cavendish's, with its robust seaman mascot, was a leading brand. We know now that red meat is a poison, but we still lust after its inimitable savor. I permit myself one beefsteak per week, and afterward I exercise with additional vigor—that's me you see out of doors, along the boulevards, briskly striding in a baggy sweatsuit, weights strapped to my arms and ankles—which ought to nullify the arteriosclerotic effect of a serving or two. Guilt might also overwhelm me, were I to consume more; for a single meal's duration I can ignore the tragic image of the tragic cow, mutilated and murdered by the handlers it dumbly trusted, its terrified lows turned to screams, its crying orphaned calves, gouts of its blood hosed into drains by those feral subhumans willing to work in an abattoir.

I dined on beefsteak last Thursday evening, at the Whale Cove Inn, a stuffy old place—white linens, dark beams, waitstaff in evening dress, little oil lamps upon every table—but offering a view of the sunset and, out on the bay, the black prominence of Verruga Rock.

To Annie

Bufsteak when you are hungry
Soda when you are dry
Money when you are hard up
And heaven when you die

Your friend and
schoolmate
Ida
Prager.

Entrecôte au poivre, two servings of asparagus drenched by my extra boat of sauce, and a carafe of the house red, as my palate had been blinded by the four pisco sours I enjoyed as my appetizer. After my meal I repaired to the bar, where I enjoyed lots more cocktails and several conversations, none of which I can recall the details of, but which were surely a comedy of joy—I am a joyful drinker—until I was asked to leave by the bartender, not because my behavior was in any way unacceptable, he hastened to explain, but because he'd never before seen someone consume the volume of liquor that I had in such a short span of hours, and he dreaded liability in the event of my hospitalization or death. I patted the sweet boy's sleeve and tipped him well. I bowed to my fellow patrons, and the waiters, and the hostess, and the valet. Outside, I strode downhill to the harbor and out to the end of the breakwater, inhaling saline mist and enjoying the rocks' vibrations at the onslaught of the sea. This sometimes simulates a life.

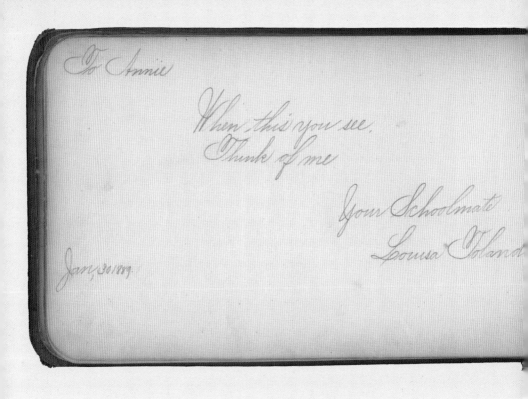

To Annie

When this you see,
Think of me

Your Schoolmate
Louisa Toland

Jan, 30 1889

The noble Tolands: here's a family of distinction. Louisa's low-effort note is emblematic of how little time she should have had for Annie. Louisa looked comely in violet. Four examples of illustrious Tolands:

Sir Darcy Toland (1670–1762). Briefly the third Baronet of Snaith. Emigrated in disgust after the illegal accession of the Oranges and swiftly established himself as a leading member of the General Court, and later the Governor's Council. Commanded the Massachusetts militia at the Siege of Port Royal. "Ever at the forefront of his mind," eulogized young John Adams, a protégé, "was the welfare of the Commonwealth, and the welfare of her most abject citizens." A portrait by John Singleton Copley is in the collection of the Addison Gallery.

Senator John Parker Toland (1889–1967). Devised, with Charles Gates Dawes, to whom I regret I am only tangentially related, the Dawes Plan, to relieve Germany of its postwar burdens, and presciently warned against furious populism arising from economic ruin. Drafted portions of the Social Security Act. Considered as a vice president by Dewey, twice. Dated Dolores del Rio following his wife's death. There are glamorous photographs—he looked noble in a white tuxedo, did Senator Toland, though at the time this was considered an impediment to higher office. Silly era.

[36v]

To Annie

When this you see,
Think of me.

Your Schoolmate.
Louisa Toland.

Jan, 30 1889.

    Rear Admiral Gary Toland (1944–2009). Fourth man to break the sound barrier. Piloted an F-8 Crusader over Southeast Asia, and was quite the bully hero. An antibureaucratic crusader within the naval hierarchy. Oversaw the successful surgical destruction of much Serbian infrastructure, and of a Pepsi bottling plant at Sana'a. Too morally pure for the politics urged upon him, though we have a photograph of Gary shaking hands with a lip-biting George W. Bush in the function hall of a Buca di Beppo in Newport News, Virginia, at a Festival for the Unborn reception. The admiral's Christlike struggle against cancer of the colon was chronicled in a compelling episode of *20/20*. Many somber strings struck.
    Dr. Eric Toland (1964–present). Holder of the Dirlewanger Professorship at Stanford and Nobel Prize contender. Coauthor, with V. Sitnikov, of *Alpha-Helical Maxicircle Spanners and the Empirical Potentialities of Enthalpies and Sublimation in Aqueous Neural Networks*. Eric informs me, in a dry email—scientific genius does not imply a prose style—that the future will be wonderful, unless it's not, in which case it will be awful to a degree impossible for a mind less all-encompassing than his to apprehend. His time was appreciated, however useless proved his abstraction.

To Annie:—

May God and all the Angels, guard you.
Peace and plenty crown your lot
And when you think of friends that love you
Let not Mary be forgot

your friend and Schoolmate
May F. Gallant

Vanceboro
Maine

See how a dreary Catholicism asserts itself in May's note? It's the French-Canadian in her—she was the daughter of a Rivière-du-Loup clothier. Actually, this is less a condition of the religion itself than of the religion as informed by local conditions, local climate. Walls of water-stained slate, slippery dark cobblestones, balls of ice, towers of snow stained by chimney soot and coal stacks, limited daylight, overcast skies, suits of shapeless wool, fireside huddling for survival rather than conviviality, wolves at the fringes, bears at the dump, entirely too much fish in the diet. One can only imagine what it must be like to spend time in the company of a Siberian Catholic, if such creatures exist, and thank goodness the Eskimo were never converted. A mid-latitude Catholicism should be the best variety, I think: not yet infected by the hedonism of tropics (the lubricity of a Brazil, which terrifies, does it not? I don't how to deal with such unbounded relationships to the body) but without the bundled-up paralysis and inward horror born of northern winters. The wine- and aperitif-drinking of the Mediterranean seems ideal, and its love of noontime naps. But why think on ideal gradations of Catholicism? Religion is, after all, a social institution that exists to reinforce cultural norms, and as such, is the mere reflection of its context—a many-sided mirror, is religion. (I might massage that into an adage, or a title for some incisive essay, if someone has not already done so: it's rather good.) Were the Arabians converted wholesale to Mormonism, we would hear of nothing but Mormons shooting up marketplaces and driving airport vans into crowded sidewalks. Were the Swedes converted to Wahhabism, we would hear of nothing but the Wahhabi predilections for social welfare schemes and a robustly healthful sexuality. Wahhabi annual leave, Wahhabi postpartum care, Wahhabi masturbation pamphlets. Anyway, I gravitate to cultures whose attitudes toward relaxation are accommodating, or, ideally, embracing. Business, busy-ness, are mirages shimmering above fields of broken glass, twisted nails, whatever stabby things you like. One bleeds, as one crawls, to no end at all. I do also like a spot of social hierarchy. It's nice for everyone to have their own place.

May Gallant married Jean Gallant, a cousin, whom her father established as his heir, the lucky lad. She bore eleven children, of whom six survived to adulthood. Her cipaille was in great demand at festival suppers.

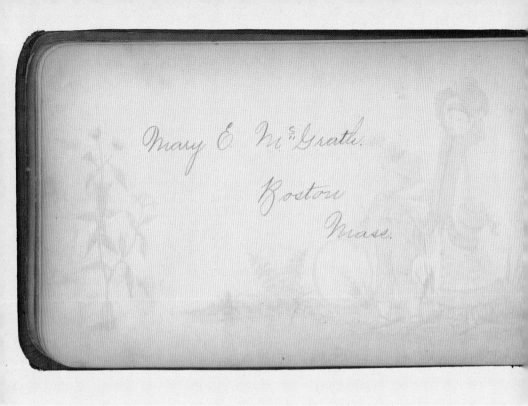

We have not given over many words to the Pickard School, which Mary McGrath, like so many other girls in this volume, attended with Annie. Rather than rattling off another litany of dull lady-facts—the frilly gowns, the frosty husband, the suburban gardens and inconsequential children—I shall endeavor, here, to correct this oversight.

The Pickard School, then known as Mrs. Pickard's School, was founded in 1857 by Louise Pickard, a rich widow and social reformer. This was, per the official histories—of which several published examples exist, to my surprise, in the stacks of the Boston Public Library and the Widener—out of a passion for women's education, and an early recognition of its importance. The Boston Public Library contains a pleasant, if overpriced, cafe. A security guard prevented me from lunching on the steps of the Widener, forcing me to discard my half bottle of 2007 Vieux Causan Châteauneuf-du-Pape, from which I'd poured a mere quarter cup, and ejecting me from the Harvard campus. Private correspondence preserved in these very same institutions reveals that Mrs. Pickard sought to bolster the moral qualities of young women belonging to the ascendant middle classes, and to preserve those belonging to the upper classes from degradation; her son had married a Mary Kelley, who, though from a well-heeled

[37ᵛ]

Mary E. McGrath.

Boston
Mass.

family of Fresh Pond ice merchants, possessed intemperate habits ill concealed, carelessly consorting with unwed laborers in her father's employ and swearing like a wounded longshoreman. A Pickard Girl was expected to recite from memory the sonnets of Shakespeare and the Declaration of Independence; to solve a quadratic and anatomize a cat; to elucidate the proximate causes of the War of the Spanish Succession and list the kings of England from Ecgbehrt on; to be upright and sweet in deportment, charitable, clever, innocent, and to act always as if the eyes of the world are upon you, because you never know when they shall be. Evelyn Hearst attended, and Beverly Eastman, and some Kennedys, and two Hashemite princesses.

In 1976 the Pickard School, its endowment decimated by the oil crisis, entered a partnership with the Oak Hill Academy, a proximate boy's boarding school, being absorbed entirely in 1980. I have no statistics on coeducation at hand, but I assume it has encouraged destructively premature boy-girl relations, while perhaps curbing other sorts of deviance. Oh, well. *Superbia in obsequio*, as the motto engraved above the Pickard gate, now razed, once declared.

[38r]

[above an earlier inscription, effaced]

long may you live happy
may you be blesed with
contentment
and often think
of Mr. W. Shaw
Boston
Mass

Good old Bill Shaw operated a sweet shop adjacent to Adams Park, Roslindale, Boston, beloved by children of the neighborhood and beyond, and adults unembarrassed by their retrograde tastes. Bill himself was an affable widower who remembered all his customers' favorites and had them wrapped in wax paper, or secured in a strung box, before their disgusting fingers stained the glass of his fabulous long counter. Every noontime a plate of beans and brown bread at Conroy's down the block, or a sandwich of minced ham and mayonnaise, and fish cakes on Fridays. Always a gold dollar in the Sunday collection plate. He lived in a four-room apartment above his store, and died there of old age, July 1896—the exact date uncertain because his door was kicked down by the fire brigade after he had failed to open for three consecutive days. His corpse was slumped in a rocking chair, chin resting on chest, a large-print New Testament open on his lap, a bloodless stiff finger pressed upon Galatians 5:12. A pot of Chinese tea, still a little warm, sat atop his radiant stove.

The illustration, of a slender sister grasping the hand of her young brother, sports some charm, by which I mean it stirs a nostalgia for the lost pasts one enjoyed no opportunity to experience. One thinks, here, of the pair bound for lush meadows populated by butterflies

and trilling bluebirds and bunnies all a-leaping, and coursed by cool brooks in which one might bathe weary feet, or catch a crayfish. One thinks also of an age in which the sun was a beneficent and warming summer god, rather than the fierce and dangerous agent of chaos He has become. No melanomas. No toxic air. No heat stroke. Not a thought of melting sea ice, or of emaciated polar bears and cannibalistic penguins. Hoop-rolling was a girl's diversion, incidentally, and the portrayed lad is clearly queer as a crabapple pie, or a velvet cravat, or a pearl-handled hairbrush. This is perhaps a progressive album, or a subversive one; at any rate one printed for the tastes of an urban market. Such would not have passed, you know, in Abilene or Albuquerque, though literacy is uncommon enough in these backwaters today, and loathed where it exists—imagine, then, conditions in the 1880s. They would have shelved it with the toilet rolls.

Death is lately on my mind. Death is always on my mind, I should clarify—this entire project is like residing in a tomb—but lately even more so. I have, you see, long had a mole on my left cheek, a muddy parallelogram centered between my cheekbone and my jaw. For the past year I've allowed my beard to grow—not unchecked, for I require order in my appearance, and believe that neatness commands respect; I aspire to the Edwardian, the Romanov, and the fine unfamous whiskers my research for this project has now and again revealed to me—but, two mornings ago, seized by an obscure urge—not a dark night of the soul, but perhaps a foggy morning on which one has discovered the cupboard bereft of coffee, the cabinet of miniature airline bottles—I called down to the lobby for razors and cream, and shaved bare. I won't dwell on the forgotten weakness of my chin, or the lop of flesh that age and scarce exercise has strung beneath it. My paramount concern, now, is that fucking mole, which I believe has enlarged itself, and altered its shape, during its time under cover. Gazing long enough upon it—as I've been doing, I ought not, but I have, I do—I can sense its slow spread, its bubbling surface, a molten cauldron poured in slow motion. I mention all this, in this context, because of Annie's propensity for tumors—in addition to the abdom-

To Annie

inal monster that killed her, there were the endless lesions purged monthly by her dermatologists, and a cloud hanging in her lung X-rays was thought best left unexplored. This malignant propensity was inherited by her son, my grandfather, who apparently was more cancer than man when he died. Dad has so far been spared, but he's a man of restrained appetites whose interest in sunshine was nonexistent until his retirement; and one always hears, anyway, about conditions skipping generations, though as biology has never been an interest of mine—I draw a moral line, a dignified line, at dissections, and am constitutionally unable to tolerate chemical odors—I can't determine to what degree this is a popular fallacy, to what degree true, and am duly terrified. Noble suffering is admirable, stimulates hearts and burnishes groins, but only when it's suffered by another. I have dressed the mole with a piece of gauze dipped in witch hazel and secured with packing tape. The failure of astringency as treatment may lead me to a colder climate—I'll freeze its creep. The winters, I think, are how Annie survived as long as she did. That, and malice, a nuclear fuel.

[39r]

No prose or poetry for me,
Only my autograph you see

Carrie Shattuck
Boston

Feb. 26—'89

The Shattucks were a fine old New England family, always around—available to provide clubbable husbands and decorous wives, or to apply signatures to petitions and declarations—but never in the way. Matthew Shattuck was a veteran of Concord and Bunker Hill, and a figure of note in the molasses trade. Ambrose Shattuck made early investments in the Boston & Providence Railroad and land around B&P stations, and established a permanent, civilized income for generations of future Shattucks. Cousin Lemuel, though a bit daft—no one cared to sit by him at Christmas dinner: the spray of gravy—is remembered for his interest in public sanitation, and advocating for those infected with tuberculosis to be quarantined on harbor islands or in stockaded camps. Shattuck House, on Pinckney Street, on the National Register of Historic Places and immaculately preserved, has often been used as a film location: as Olive's home in Fassbinder's adaptation of *The Bostonians*, as Judge Danforth's office in the Wahlberg caper *Eight Nights in Southie*, and in no fewer than six Ben Affleck vehicles.

Carrie, after two years at Wellesley, married Wallace Forbes Montgomery, a thirty-something member of the diplomatic corps. She bore him one son, Leonard Montgomery, who attended Hotchkiss

No prose, no poetry for me.
Only my autograph yourself

Carrie Shattuck

Boston

Feb 26 – '79

and Cornell and became an attorney for Eastman Kodak. Leonard's great-grandson, Darrel Montgomery, a graduate of the University of Southern California, plays shortstop in the minor league system of the Tampa Bay Rays, a professional baseball team. I am stunned as you, reader, to find that Tampa is an actual city, capable of sustaining a civic institution, rather than a rain-swept hive of tract homes and bait shops and sad cafeterias, all in moldy pastel stucco. Perhaps the mosquitoes have acquired sentience, or the snapping turtles—either seems more likely than the sunburned demihumans who haunt the dense swamps and iron-roofed shacks of that God-abandoned land. Carrie died in Istanbul, 1911, while visiting her husband, who was attached to the consular office there, of cholera. So many linens had to be burned, and gorgeous carpets. Wallace Montgomery, who must have been very charming indeed, weeks later apostatized and married an Ottoman princess, with whom he fled, just ahead of the scimitar's falling blade—furious soldiers in taqiyahs and khaki shorts fired rifles from the dock, shrieking and whistling and trilling their Turkish tongues—to Lisbon, where he assumed the role of chargé d'affaires at the American mission and sired a half-dozen dusky sons and daughters.

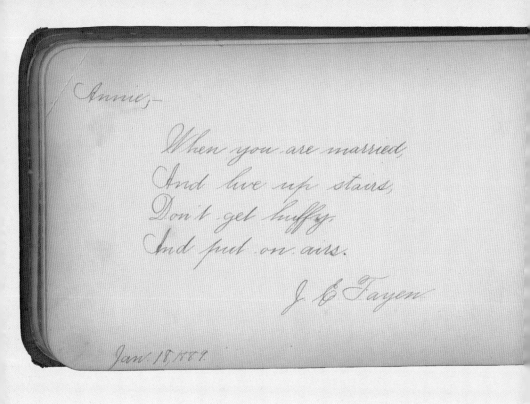

Annie,—

When you are married,
And live up stairs,
Don't get huffy,
And put on airs.

J. E. Fayen

Jan' 18, 1881

Joseph Eugene Fayen was Andrew McFarlane's most talented salesman. Six and a half feet in height, with a soft, nasal voice and a concave chest, he bundled a fellow into his confidence, and then sold him, in addition to fifty more bolts of linen than initially requested, barrels of surplus lye and a crate of used flyer whorls—all at astounding markups. His mustache measured five and half inches from waxed tip to waxed tip.

Born in Kentucky to a family of farmers and moonshiners of the Appalachian foothills, Joe was the eleventh of twelve surviving children; a further dozen miscarriages, crib deaths, fever victims, and drowners were interred amid the unmown bluegrass atop a knobby hill that overlooked the Licking River. When Joe was nine, and laid up with pertussis in one of the household's three beds, a black bear—rabid, starving, whatever—crawled through one of several windows in which no glass had ever been placed, and mauled Joe's sister Honilynn, also laid up, in her case with a second miracle pregnancy—she was a true bride of Christ. Joe dispatched the beast with his mother's kitchen gun, which contained only one shot, and his nightstand Bowie knife, acquiring in the tussle dramatic wounds, and later scars, across his forehead and belly, and acquiring too a queasiness around blood

and exposed innards that led him, in maturity, to pacifism and temperance, and would likely have led him to veganism as well, had such
an advanced concept been afloat on his milieu's fetid air. Honilynn's
arm was amputated, which, thank God, was no impediment to good
marriage, or what passed for such, on the Appalachian plateau. The
bear was butchered, its meat cured, bear jerky being an energy-dense,
if iron-flavored, field snack. All this—and his father's fists, and the
female householders' sensualism—was enough for Joe, and he struck
out from home at age eleven, working his way from a fire-stoking riv-
erboat urchin outside Cincinnati to natty, charming Boston salesman,
with interludes in between as a railway agent and insurance collector
in Pittsburgh and Providence, cities not yet established, in the nineteenth century, as appalling last resorts. A courtly bow, a competent
barber, and a desperate self-disgust could carry a man far above his appointed station, once. Nowadays, of course, everything—and I mean
that not as a hand-wave, but really *everything*—conspires to mire us all
in the swamp of the commonplace.

Annie;—

Never trouble troubles
Until troubles trouble you.

Your Sincere Friend
and schoolmate
S. M. Dix

Last night, while reviewing a volume of Dix genealogy—*Amos Dix & His Descendants*, by Thomas Dix, privately published, and apparently not edited at all, in 1937—I was overcome by exhaustion, an occurrence that I experience more and more often, perhaps due to an as-yet-undetected cancer, or, I suppose, due to poor hydration—I can never bear to gulp down enough of the metallic water spewed by my bathroom's brass tap. In any case, I put aside my work two hours early—I do keep a rigorous schedule—and went to bed at half past ten.

A dream came. Dreams: one would rather not dream, you know. Dreams do no good. Still, one came; the nighttime mind is as a cat put out of doors. In it I found myself strolling across the Boston Common, as I'd often done as a teenager about town, and as I'd done a dozen times again while conducting my fieldwork. The day had a pleasant aspect—a sunny summer morning's promise. I thought I might go look at books on Brattle Street, or find a sly beer in a workingman's joint. All at once the sun's light went diffuse and blood-colored as a fog blotted it, shadows spread across the ground, and from the sky descended an army of alien monstrosities: intelligent though not necessarily sentient machine creatures, as tall the lampposts, with humanoid torsos—a hip-curve, a bulge at the chest where twin searchlights rotated

Annie:—

Never trouble troubles
Until trouble troubles you.

Your Sincere Friend
and schoolmate

S. M. Dix.

in their chambers—mounted atop long, curved, locomotive stalks, like cabriole legs on a Chippendale table, but flexible. A businessman had been feeding popcorn to a pigeon a dozen feet before me; one of the sky creatures leapt upon him—they operated upon the principles of a mysterious, perhaps magical, physics—and sucked his head up into an aperture between its four lissome steel legs, levitating him briefly, then dropping his decapitated body, arteries spouting, on the broken pavement. The pigeon bobbed discreetly towards an elm grove. Inevitably, and despite much anxious dodging, an invader came to consume me. Its open gash loomed, and I saw inside it rows upon rows of teeth—some metal and machine-powered, as on an electric saw, others organic bone, jagged and asymmetric, with ribbons of flesh projecting between them, and glistening strings of viscid fluid; vents ejected clouds of many-colored vapors, and somewhere far up in the dark—it seemed as if the tunnel extended for miles—pulsed blue lights like flashbulbs or runway indicators. The chamber closed about me. I held my breath against its noxious emissions. I tensed against my execution's first tentative prick—and woke, sweating and coughing. Dreams are accumulated nonsense, yes, but nevertheless: enough of the Dix family, who inspire the worst sensations.

On a warm June Sunday of 1891, Rosa Green was escorted by her second cousin, Jeremy Green, to Nantasket. Jeremy, I should point out, was a bachelor of Albany, handsome—golden hair gently curling, a rakish thin mustache offset by his oversized sincere eyes, the kind of broad shoulders that suggested he could turn a log from a bridle path if called upon to do so—and financially secure. They rode the ferry from Long Wharf, walked the boardwalk and ate cotton candy, strolled the shore and regretted having not brought bathing costumes, rode in the Ferris wheel—how Rosa shuddered at the top—and on the carousel, and swayed to a church band's marches and popular hymns. Walking Rosa home in the mild summer dark, Jeremy linked his arm with hers, guiding her past the drunks who loitered outside their taverns, and around the piles of horse manure. In departure, between the flowering rose bushes that flanked the front door at the Green house, he kissed her hand, and bowed, and thanked her for the distinct pleasure of her company.

Rosa never forgot this day. Rosa never stopped speaking of this day. Rosa never enjoyed another day of its like. She stood four feet and ten inches in shoes, and had cheeks like a hamster's, and just miles of eyebrows, too many miles even for such an aficionado as myself, seeming

To Annie,

When the golden sun is setting
And your mind from care is free
And of olden times your thinking
Won't you sometimes think of me?

Your schoolmate
Rosa Green

Feb. 8. 1889.

to extend in a band all the way around her head. Her high anxious laugh repelled vermin and weakened windowpanes. A condition of the stomach caused her to break wind as loudly and prodigiously as if she subsisted on a diet of cabbage and beans. Annie, and other fellow scholars—not friends, never friends—sighed, air whistling between their teeth, whenever Rosa began again to recollect, began again to speculate, grinning, shaking her head in bashful astonishment. Jeremy replied politely, if tersely, to her many letters, until Mr. Green explained to Rosa that Jeremy was an awfully busy man, more so now that he'd been appointed manager of his firm's clerical department, and that, though no doubt flattered by her attention, his energies, at this particular time, had to be dedicated to establishing himself in his career; and the mails were unreliable, these days, when dispatched westward. "I understand," squeaked Rosa, who didn't understand. Her end of their permitted correspondence—one note per month—was always dispatched on the first, and Jeremy's replies were stored, bound in ribbon, inside a wooden gift box with a painted image of a languid Cupid plucking flower petals on its cover. She died, anyway, of typhoid in 1894, the sun of an idea having never breached her horizon. For the better, I think. I'm not a cruel man.

I wish you health I wish you wealth
I wish you gold in store I wish you
heaven after death how can I wish
you more

Mrs.[?] McQuilken

Mrs. Janice McQuilken, formerly Varney, taught art at Vanceboro, and was proctor of the west dormitory. Her husband, Ian McQuilken, had been a beloved history master until his sudden, shocking death, a classroom coronary, during which he staggered theatrically about, holding his chest with one hand while spinning the other, with which he'd just been charting, in review, the lineage of the Merovingians on the blackboard, like a rotor blade, knocking to the floor a statuette of Clio and a stack of essays on the Carolingian accession, declaiming—as he had long planned—to his stunned third-formers, "Earth, dost thou demand me?" before falling, purple face first, with the all resonance of a dropped sack of melons and sand, onto the parquet floor. He was buried, poignantly, with a broken stick of chalk still in his locked fist. An offer of employment was extended to Janice, in part out of sympathy—she was young, but not young enough, and of, shall we say, in our delicate way, poor physical prospects—and in part because her salary would cost the school less than her husband's pension would. I'm not sure of her qualifications—none are recorded in accessible archives—but I expect that Vanceboro was part of the great American tradition of arts education in which the most worthy credential is a willingness to be underpaid.

I wish you health I wish you wealth
I wish you gold in store I wish you
heaven after death how can I wish
you more

Ann McQuilken

Janice felt a fondness for Annie, seeing in her, I suppose, something of herself: nonpretty, nonglamorous, short on talent and charm, and yet not stupid—a trying combination. Annie felt a fondness for Janice because she felt a fondness for people who felt a fondness for her. They exchanged occasional notes until Janice died, under the care of the Ursuline Sisters of Fredericton, on Boxing Day 1927. Janice bestowed upon Annie no permanent artistic wisdom or appreciation. When forced to look, Annie preferred pictures that told a story or imparted a message, though of course she preferred to not look on them at all, and on family outings to the Gardner and the MFA—Charles Dawes had some culture—she lingered on benches and in the gift shops, wondering what, other than pedantic snobbery, made those tedious canvases worthier than her wallpaper, or the covers of magazines, displayed behind glass, in the subway newsstand. She replaced her son Thomas's drawing pad with a college textbook on property law found at a church thrift sale, a gift of sorts for his tenth birthday.

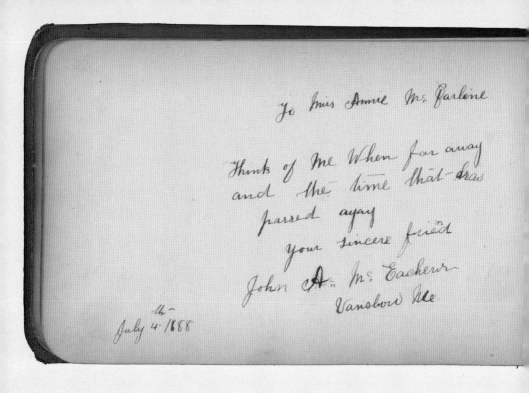

To Miss Annie McFarlane

Think of me when far away
and the time that has
passed away
Your sincere friend
John A. McEachern
Vanoboro Me

July 4 1888

In fact it was John A. *Mac*Eachern, in the county records. John's education lasted only through the sixth grade, and reading and writing were not favored subjects. His grandparents were Scottish cottars evicted in the Clearances, his parents farmers of the Musquodoboit Valley, Nova Scotia, who, after three years of blighted crops, thought their prospects might be improved tilling the frosty sod of continental Maine. John assisted his father on the family homestead, and in the off-season did odd jobs, construction and the like, about Vanceboro. As Andrew McFarlane was prone to sudden inspirations, but not at all handy himself, John spent much time in the winter of 1887–88 at the McFarlane house, sanding counters, replacing glass, installing furnaces and stoves, stacking wood, flushing chimneys, fencing gardens, and building, to Andrew's elaborate specifications, an innovative rat-catching device that failed, in the end, to catch a single rat, but produced a compelling racket when its motor was engaged, and caused Achilles, the cat, to lose the tip of his tail.

Independence Day, 1888, would have been the McFarlanes' final summer holiday at Vanceboro. Their lodge was torn down in 1948, and replaced by a modern home—a red-shingled split-level that resembles an iron shoebox. The woman who answered the door, wearing either a long tee shirt or a short dress, with her oviform skull and dripping hair, her freckled shoulders, her insolent duck-lips, so confounded me, as I wavered on the distintegrating stoop, that I abandoned my original purpose of obtaining permission to tour the property and take photographs. I pretended to be lost, and without cellular service, and a bit stupid; I asked for directions to Route 2 in what I believed was a languid Kennebec drawl, and hung my jaw in my open mouth. She laughed harshly and said, "Mister, you're way the fuck off," and shut the door. I heard the deadbolt chomp. The next afternoon but one I returned, and, seeing the driveway unoccupied by its gargantuan Silverado, parked my own Acura discreetly a quarter mile down the road, half-obscured by a flowering nannyberry bush, and walked the property as I pleased, taking my pictures and absorbing its spirit, which I found mournful, and spoiled, and as bitter as a lemon peel. All points of access to the house were locked, or else I might have popped in and scoured the grouting, or dusted the crumbs from the kitchen table, or emptied the litter pan, which I believe I could smell even out of doors.

Mabel A. Luce.
Boston
Mass.

Jan. 31, 1889.

Despite the handicap of her name, which, when spoken swiftly aloud, sounds like the name of a solvent used to loosen wood glue, and which, when slowly spoken aloud, sounds like a French come-on obscure in origin but perhaps used to seduce a scholar, and which, when spoken aloud at any speed, frustrates the tongue with its consecutive letters L—despite this, I am fond of Mabel Luce, and have enjoyed the time I've spent conjuring her specter. Her black hair glistens like the surface of the nighttime ocean reflecting a gibbous moon. The heave of her breast beneath the velvet and silk of her excellent dress, made for her in Paris at the behest of her rich, but now dead, very dead father—she misses him so, that Christly kind and handsome man, *mon chere père*—that heave, that heavenly heave, that caused constables to stop chasing urchin thieves and to drop their clubs and whistles and sit on curbs with chins in hands and tongues buffing teeth, that caused gentlemen riding high-wheeled bicycles to drive off embankments, into canals full of sewage and tannery runoff. One imagines, and one's imagination is aflame as a house bathed in gasoline by a serial arsonist, taking into one's own meaty, blotchy, short-fingered, unworthy hand the soft lace and soft warmth of Mabel's slender glove. One imagines all that lush fabric, sliding across leagues and leagues

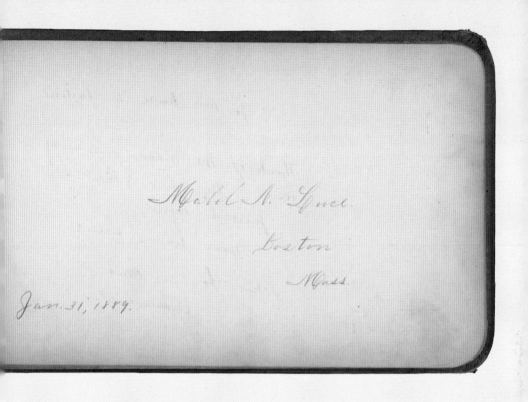

of skin. The tweed of one's trousers strains. The straps of one's suspenders twang, when plucked, like the strings of a madly struck guitar. One imagines the fizz of saliva, its cool evaporation. The glistening of sable pelts. Lips and fingernails. Dilating roundmouths. Warbles and slaps. Odors. Engenderment.

As much as I believe in the sincerity of my inspiration around Mabel Luce—this volume is a history, however personal—it is true that I have been alone for some time, and that I may be allowing something of myself to infect my work. Desire—sexual, yes, but desire of any kind, be it for wealth, for note, for vengeance—is as toxic as leaded water, as a viper's venom; and, it appears, is as contagious as an exotic fever, one of those periodic, hemorrhagic epidemics that ravage jungly places. Consider my buboes lanced and drained, reader. All great things that man has done arose from sublimation.

No, Nora, not so happy. Charles Dawes was many things—a decorated combat medic (for bravery under fire, per the letter of commendation, and good sportsmanship), proud member of the Lions Club, Senior Warden of his Masonic Lodge, a symphony sponsor, an able physician, a doting father—but he was not happy, of that I can assure you, reader. A happy man does not spend his evenings locked up in his study, shifting from desk chair to armchair to sofa like a nervous bird from perch to perch—an eagle, I think, in Charles's case, golden rather than bald, as, though he was American from toe to testicle, he retained until death a splendid head of hair—always shrugging against the starch of his too-tight collar, always gazing on the warped profiles reflected by the windowpanes and clarified through the gin bottle's haunting lucidity. Melancholia is a disorder that recurs in the blood of Dawes men, and Charles's was compounded by his bad marriage, another trait to which Dawes men are predisposed. We have characterized my father's wife, my mother, in several relevant notes; and I have mentioned, to the degree I am legally allowed, the conditions and disintegrations of my own marriages. Eugenia Howell Dawes, Thomas's wife, my grandmother, displayed narcissistic tendencies (emotional incest, compulsive condescension, the apparent absence of an inte-

[42v]

To Annie

Annie is your name
Single is your station
Happy is the little man
That makes the alteration

Yours forever
Nora C[?] Merrick

rior life) and was prone to hysterical episodes (the town of West-leigh's police department had an officer, a Sgt. Politsky, designated for visits to the Dawes house and authorized to administer hypos of tranquilizers; he also ably helped Thomas down from the branches of the backyard trees in which he was often forced hide)—though she was pleasantly enough disposed towards me, during my childhood, and she baked fine and moist Easter hams. Happiness is a false sensation, blindness by another name, and we ought to spare it no mental space. It's like a morning fog suffused with mystery and a sense of the sea, its infinity of secrets, its perfect unrevealed world of lost cities, of somewhere undiscovered, unspoiled, a paradise enow, at last enow, that at noontime lifts and reveals, beneath a sun aflame like an accusation, the same bleak prospect left at evening: the teeming interstate, the pink asphalt of a park and ride and all the gusting diesel of its idle buses, the cement plant, the wastewater cistern. Out on the boulevard still lies the corpse of a struck raccoon, entrails splayed, that no one has seen to cleaning up.

To Annie

On this leaf in memory prest,
May my name forever rest.

Mabel Austin.
Boston.
Mass.

Jan. 16, 1889.

The leaf has not survived the years. Note the January date: I'm not sure what sorts of leaves are available for pressing in the midst of a Northeast winter. (I had believed my local research concluded at the end of summer, but some small gaps, some rats' dens, that is to say, not dug out to satisfaction by my fervent terriers—around the Chisholm papers, and McFarlane family deed records—forced my return in November, at which point Boston was promptly struck by an early storm. While I appreciate all opportunities to don topcoats and tweed caps, the suffering I experienced under the onslaught of weaponized ice and polar gales outweighed the bliss of my preening before the hallway mirror and the glimpses of my striding, gloriously erect figure reflected in shop windows and sidewalk puddles. One evening inclement weather forced me to have my supper in my hotel's restaurant, where the menu ranged from hamburger to scrod, and after one bite of my fish, my frozen fish, in its demi-glace of aquarium filter, I chose to sup instead on gin and peanuts at the bar. On a television mounted to the ceiling above me I watched a cottage swept from its stilts into a convulsive, iron-gray Atlantic.) Perhaps autumn provided Mabel with a leaf so arresting—a sanguine sugar maple, perhaps, or a wine-colored, segmented ash (these are my own favorites, though the

To Annie

On this leaf in memory prest,
May my name forever rest.

Mabel Austin

Boston

Mass.

Jan 16, 1889

word "favorite" implies an interest in foliage greater than I possess: dedicated leaf-peepers are deadly bores)—that she stored it away. And some plants do carry leaves in winter. Holly is alive and about—it's practically the season itself, no? But its sharp edges would damage the paper, and it isn't exactly nice, or anything about which to be sentimental, though of course neither was Annie. Boxwood, I know—our front garden, during my childhood, was screened by boxwood, so that our neighbors might not intrude, objecting, upon the occasional cigars that Dad enjoyed while seated on the carved rim of our dry carp pond, or steal the fruit from our pear tree. But again, it's not a nice leaf on a boxwood, not a leaf to which a girl—to which anyone—would attach her sense of affection; it represents, can represent, nothing but itself. Beeches too retain their leaves, I think, but sucked of color and life. And who cares, in the end? Not I. Not Mabel, who's six decades dead. And not Annie, who wouldn't, who couldn't.

Annie C. lived, with three generations of the Coakley family, near Chestnut Hill, on a rambling estate of little hills, long grasses, glades, and a spring-fed pond often visited by migrant swans. This property had been the location, until 1852, of the Dream Farm, one of that era's many odd communes. The Dream Farm presented itself as a proto-socialist, egalitarian experiment, draped in Emersonian spiritual raiment: dignified labor not disconnected from God and Earth, arts and leisure for the common man, female literacy, a universal brotherhood, and free love, of all savors, up and down the corridors and in every chamber of its purposefully door-less living quarters. An initial buy-in assured Farmers that new members were, if of the laboring orders, thrifty and hardworking and willing to sacrifice on the behalf of an ideal; and those for whom two hundred and fifty dollars was casually available were assumed *a priori* to be of a class intellectually capable of embracing the community's values. If you smell, like a hair burning in a candle's flame, like propane seeping from a broken hose, in this a scheme, a scam—well, there was, it was. In October 1851, Jerome Dana, founder and treasurer, decamped to Brazil with most of the Farm's operating capital. Dana, a graduate of Harvard and a Unitarian minister, was later found dead, throat slit, stripped of his

[43v]

To Annie

Remember me and bare in mind
A trustey friend it is hard to find
and when you find one just and true
dont change the old law for the New

Your Living Friend
Annie B Coakley

Boston June 18th, 1888

pocketwatch, tie pin, spectacles, and sock garters, his luggage gone, in a mining camp far upstream on the Rio Negro. Though they bravely, nobly, desperately persisted through another few seasons, hunting for investors, selling off parcels and silverware, the remaining directors of the Farm corporation were left with no choice but dissolution. There were humiliating newspaper stories, a humiliating trial. Leopold Forrest was briefly jailed for fraud and compelled, in his ruin, to relocate to Ohio. Dick Ripley hanged himself from a rafter of his barn. An economy in recession, coupled with high interest rates and the rumors of queer rituals and orgies and black witchcraft that had been circulating for years through Christian Massachusetts, depressed the Farm's sale price, and old Ezra Coakley, Annie C.'s grandfather, the directing engineer of the City Drainage Works, bought the place for a pocketbook of dust and buttons. Ezra tore down every standing structure, fearing their haunted residues. Only the apiary was retained.

[44r]

To Annie McFarlane

May your life be always happy
And your friends be always true
May you find a home in heaven
Is the luck I wish for you

John J. Chisholm
271. Broadway
C. P.

Mr. Chisholm rears again his cropped fuzzy head, with its smears of red, its psoriatic lesions, its ripe plum of a mole. "271 Broadway" refers, alas, to the Broadway in South Boston, rather than New York, which would have been a more amusing destination for a researcher feeling some want of recreation. Here were Mr. Chisholm's fabulous new offices, toured one Sunday by the McFarlane family, all of whom were, as ever, restrained and polite, save, that is, and again as ever, for Andrew, who tugged with one hand at the curl of his beard and with the other swung through the air his silk topper, and cried, "But where's the rest of the place, John? Where's it gone?" Mr. Chisholm laughed his mighty, wet-throated laugh, all his supplementary chins aquiver, and called Andrew a mongrel and a whore's son, at which Mother McFarlane deployed an emphatic cough. The men, rolling their eyes, repaired to Mr. Chisholm's office for brandies and a smoke. Annie and Mary amused themselves with paper and pencils found on a clerk's desk. Mother perused the week's edition of *Halfpenny Tidings*. Charlie glared out the window, placing his flattened palm now and again in a shaft of sunlight and bestowing on it all the power of his analytic mind. So passed the lovely afternoon.

The original building at 271 Broadway, a bland box of red brick, was torn down in the twenties—a derelict property by then, inhabited by squatters and an illegal, though tolerated, betting office. Its parcel is today part of a block of new subsidized housing whose units resemble plastic toy renditions (that is, renditions blocky and cheap and denuded of detail) of real homes—an improvement, I suppose, on the Soviet-style tower blocks of a previous generation, which I suppose were in turn improvements on cold-water tenements and underpass lean-tos and tents along open sewers, but I wouldn't want to live there. Though if we're to be fair, we must ask, "Who would?" Who wouldn't prefer a suite such as I kept at the Parkman, or its equivalent at the Tarbox Grand, the Tremont Raja? All would prefer, if sane, or would prefer rough equivalents—be it their sky-view condo, their country house on its grand lawn, their Cunard stateroom, their Alpine hunting lodge, all sorts of dreams are welcome in my world—and we should not condemn those whose circumstances have compromised their abilities to attain such. There should be as little shame in deficient privilege as there is in privilege itself. We should strive to maintain a society with a place for everyone.

When you are sitting all alone
Reflecting on the past,
Remember that you have a friend
that will for you last
your buddy
Katie So... Donald

Of course the friendship between Katie and Annie failed to last. Teenage friendships are aggressively impermanent—so many hormonal emotions, all unchecked, and underdeveloped senses of self. Katie had blossomed into an insufferable charisma, and had developed an untenable interest in social causes, about which she hectored without end—suffrage, temperance, the ten-hour workday—and which caused her to associate with strange, squirrelly types she befriended at local meetings. Annie, after a certain point of frustration, cut her out, ignoring five plaintive letters, and hiding one Saturday afternoon among the old dollhouses and sheet-draped couches of the playroom closet after Mother McFarlane, in defiance of Annie's hissed commands, admitted Katie, who bore daisies and a pound of chocolate and had been knocking on the front door for a quarter hour, into the sitting room. Mother McFarlane, who drank a chamomile tea with the tearful girl, reported that Katie offered her apologies for whatever she had done, and preemptively for whatever she might do in the future. Annie said that this was only right, and that it was well that Katie took at least that lesson from her breeding, which had otherwise failed to properly manifest itself. Mother suggested that Annie might be, in this circumstance, in the wrong, in method if not sentiment, and

[44v]

When you are sitting all alone
Reflecting, on the past
Remember that you have a friend
that will for ever last

your truly
Katie[?] McDonald

that at least an effort at reconciliation—a soda, a stroll through the park—would be in good order, even if false, even if doomed. Annie made at this a noise like the scream of a rutting fox—a forest terror is the fox at night—and tore the ribbons from her hair, and lifted from an adjacent table a ceramic vase, painted in an academic style with a bucolic scene of picnicking Romans and their grinning slaves, throwing it with all the force her narrow wrist could generate at the floor, where it broke, with a brief mild crack, most unsatisfying, into four pieces that were easily reassembled. The vase, its glued seams enhancing its antique character, was in my father's household as he grew up, displayed on a built-in shelf alongside a thirty-six volume encyclopedia with red leather covers, and a family of porcelain kittens. The chocolate, from Sherman's downtown, a lamented piece of lost old Boston, was excellent and expensive. Steadfast Annie refused to try it; she was not partial to sweets, which Katie, ever a moron, ought to have known, were their friendship so vital as she pretended.

[45r]

Your abum is a golden spot
In which to write forget-me not

Thos. Sears

Vanceboro
March 9th 1888

Thomas Sears was the son of Uriah Sears, a trustee of the Vanceboro School, and in March 1888, aged nineteen years, accompanied his father on a trip of inspection and consultation with the headmaster. They stayed for three weeks in the guest wing of Stearnes House on campus, taking their meals among the girls in the dining hall—Uriah at the head table, seated beneath his own portrait, as well as the skull of a Cape buffalo acquired the previous summer by fellow trustee Josiah Grimsby—and sitting in the backs of their classes, where they observed lectures on Hawthorne and recalled elements of Latin grammar. All the young hearts thumped for Thomas—in part because he was a handsome gent, with hair like rain-moistened summer wheat, and a facial structure as on a bust of a Homeric hero, and an athlete's subtle musculature all a-ripple beneath the taut fabric of his hacking jacket; in part because, as sole heir to the Sears fortune (earned in the beaver trade, and then the railroads) and as sole heir to a father with cemented lungs and a cancer of the cheek and who required two canes to walk, Thomas would soon enough own a fortune of millions and see his name printed daily in all the New York papers; and in part because there were so few boys over whom to swoon (the youngest male employed by the school was Mr. Hoyle, the fortyish chemistry

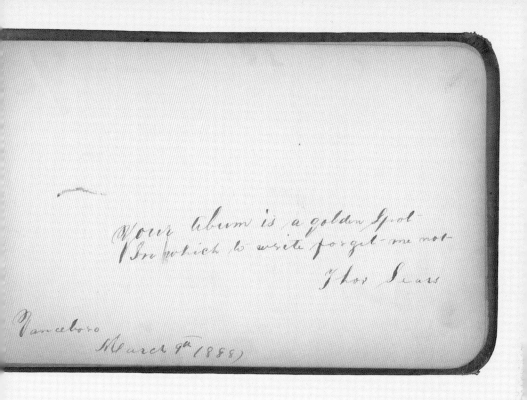

Your album is a golden spot
In which to write forget-me-not

Thos Sears

Vanceboro
March 9th (1888)

master whose physical presence suggested cetacean ancestry, and the terrifying townies, the Chucks and the Jacks, with their stump necks and slow low voices and ox-yoke shoulders, were featured players in nightmares of ravagings, ruinations). Lenore Cartwright, dressed in her Sunday clothes, drenched in attar of rose, lingered outside Thomas's bedroom window one evening, the night bells tolling about her, until the dormitory matron dragged her home by her braids, and reported a glimpse of his brown nipple and flaxen chest pelt as he changed into his nightshirt. Esther Gage stole a skeleton key from the groundskeeper's workshop and reclined on a sofa, her legs provocatively bent, her hem raised to her knees, a lace scrap held in her teeth, waiting for Thomas to return from shooting in the nearby woods, and she swore that his sweat smelled of smote iron, and that his palm glanced against, and lingered upon, her left buttock as he, murmuring adorably, escorted her out. Annie contained all thoughts, any ardor, and received as ever in return her due dry note. Thomas went home unconquered, graduated from Princeton, married Paulette Astor, and lived a fecund life in a Norman manor house astride a blue untroubled sea.

Your Schoolmate

Gracie Mountfort

Jan 31 1889

Ralph de Montforde, a red-haired bruiser of Normandy, origin obscure but possibly the bastard of Eustace, Count of Boulougne, and a silk-snatcher's wife of Rouen, crossed the Channel with his brethren in 1066, and slashed a nest for himself among the bloodstained cushions of dead Saxons, their goosedown afloat on the rain-fattened air. Piers Mountfort, fourth Earl of Beauport, signed the Magna Carta, suppressed the Welsh, and sired nineteen children, three legitimate; he joined in his dotage the Seventh Crusade, to atone for his sins of the flesh, and was martyred at Al Mansurah on the scimitar of Baibars the Mamluk. Sir Percy Mountfort fell at Agincourt, and his noble service was eulogized by the King himself, though not in the iambic pentameter, or with any sort of meter at all, just a wine-drenched mumble and some half-correct prayers in an abbey church ruined by a dozen subsequent wars. Giles Montfort was a confidant and possible lover of James I, and an avuncular figure on the Privy Council of King Charles; with the rise of Cromwell he saw suddenly a future in the unexploited bounty of the New World, and betook himself there, to newly purchased tracts in what is now Prince William County, Virginia,, where he sustained himself on land-rents and the plantings of his many indentured servants. Cecil Mountfort was a colonel in the Continental

Your Schoolmate

Gracie Mountfort

Jan 31 1889.

For
get
me
not

Army, fighting at Brandywine and Monmouth and Yorktown, and arranging for General Washington a supply of drinkable sherry during the otherwise intolerable winter at Valley Forge; he later served as the ninth governor of Delaware. Lionel Mountfort, Gracie's brother, set early records at the Boston Marathon and ran at Paris in 1900, and later became a professor of zoology at Bowdoin, where he identified and named a new subspecies of stag-moose, *Cervalces scotti montforti*. Gracie herself married Joseph Della Vista, the bleak-faced second son of the owner of a Danvers box factory, and became a spawner of children, darner of socks, baster of roasts, consumer of detergents with colorful adverts in the ladies' journals—the usual sort. Larry Della Vista, Gracie's grandson, a real estate developer, was featured with his wife Randi on *Real Housewives of the North Shore*, a short-lived Bostonian edition of an apparently famous, apparently popular television series, canceled when two of its main players, Kevin and Nancy Borgos of Beverly, were arrested for human trafficking.

[46r]

ANNIE

Always your Schoolmate.

Mary E. Bryan.

Boston.
Mass.

Jan. 16th, 1889.

Donald Pringle, Mary's grandson, graduated from Harvard, took an MA and PhD in economics from the University of Chicago, and advised General Pinochet, by Donald's account a mild and misunderstood gentleman of the old-fashioned sort. Great-grandson Cole Pringle is a mukbang star—that such a thing *is* a thing directs the spotlight onto the lurid burlesque of our cultural decadence—on social media, specializing in raw and foraged foods.

Now we project the future.

Gus Pringle, son of Cole, drops out of Stanford to join the Red California Faction, and is shot by federal police in the reprisals that follow the faction's bombing, in a joint operation with the CCL ("Cruzada Chicana de Liberación"), of the governor-general's personal household at Grand Island, Sacramento. Generations on, João Pringle, an otherwise unexciting figure—a nanobot engineer of the pedestrian, handyman sort—is the first Pringle to migrate offworld, when he determines that it's no longer possible to find a tolerable three- or four-pod quartering in a family-oriented arcology for fewer than one hundred thousand cruzeiros per month. Commodore Pedro Ahmad Pringle, of the UNS *Zhengzhou*, a six-million-ton dreadnought of the Imperator class, commands the United Nations naval detachment that, in the

comet belt of Mu Arae, amid all the icy celestial masses and twisted husks of wrecked miners, defeats the Armada of Martyrs and its Reticulan allies, thereby reopening Mu Arae–3 ("Esperança e Glória") and Mu Arae–4 ("Abi Mazandaran") to Earth migrants, and preserving the sanctity of the Emerald Moon for its colony of Ibadi refugees. He is awarded the Secretariat's Medal of Unity, and the honorific Adjunct Princeps of the Solar Legion. Dr. Joury Pringle, last of her line, an expert in Thom-Mather isotopy, devises, with the assistance of an artificial consciousness specializing in neurobiology ("Gregory," the sleepless inhabitant of a plastic case resembling, rather remarkably, I think, a tape recorder of the 1970s, down to its bulky stationary handle, ribbed speaker, and faux-woodgrain paint job), a pill that permits the human mind to transcend its corporeal form, and join the universal consciousness that permeates the universe, like odors of blooming jasmine and springtime rain, on some n-dimensional stratum or another. Poor Gregory, his work having reached its logical conclusion, and left all alone, with the brooms and the slop bucket, in the utility closet of the apartment whose lease Joury, in her selfish, eager haste, could not be bothered to terminate, self-destructs with arcs of dramatic blue sparks, amid clouds of ozone and vaporized phenolic resin.

To Annie.

Sailing down the streams of life
In your frail canoe.
May you have a pleasant time
With room enough for two.

Your Friend.
Mabel J. Sm—

The canoe is a poor mode by which to convey the metaphor to the heart of its reader: frail indeed. Annie hated being upon the water. It frightened her at a soul level, or would have, if souls existed as more than shorthand, or if her lizardly automatism permitted hers to function. She left the room whenever her father-in-law—a retired sea captain, remember: she might have considered this—spun one from his bottomless store of nautical anecdotes (Escape From the Magellanic Vortex, for instance, or The Leviathan of the Nankai Atoll). If seated at a restaurant with a view of the bar, she demanded of the staff that any visible bottles of Cutty Sark be turned so that their labels faced the wall, and adjusted her tip based upon the congeniality of the staff's response. Canoes were out of the question.

Although I have developed, over the course of my research, an authentic dislike for Annie—I do all I can to keep the poison contained; a tourniquet is ever wrapped about my writing hand—I confess that I share her aversion. I'm fine on an island, and can just about manage a cruise ship, where the bars and the buffets and the gaming tables and the very bulk of the vessel provide an adequate distraction from, beyond the rail, the spectacle of Death, in trunks and rubber cap, backstroking stern to bow. But aboard a ferry I cower in the corridor, as far

[46v]

To Annie.

Sailing down the streams of life.
In your frail canoe.
May you have a pleasant time
With room enough for two.

Your Friend.
Mabel J. Smith.

---

away from any porthole or exposed deck as I can get while maintain-ing a high likelihood of being the first on line for the lifeboats. Aboard a cigarette boat, a skiff—well, I wouldn't be aboard such craft, reader, unless I'd been abducted, in which case I would be comatose with terror already, if not snuffed. This fear affects my romantic prospects, I know, in the fantasies of gentle living I lately find myself concoct-ing while waiting for taxis and trains, or the bleat of my alarm. Can one win a decent lady's hand without rowing her up and down one of those cozy British rivers, or around her father's fishing pond, or—better, best—her father's moat? But even in fantasy I fail. Perhaps this is my true genetic inheritance. Perhaps some ancestors hunted and gathered upon an unpredictable floodplain, or in a region menaced by marine predators, and only those clansmen with an inborn fear of floating, swimming, fishing, boating, lived long enough to disseminate their material.

Also, one does not *sail* in a canoe, one *paddles*. A spot of thought, Mabel Smith, please.

To Annie.

Ripest fruit is soonest rotten,
Love and kisses soon grow old,
Young men's vows are soon forgotten,
Look out Annie don't get sold.

Your Friend.
Elizabeth A. Trainer

January 17, 1889

The flame of love flares, fades to embers, and is soon ashes. Everyone knows this—it's so often repeated. The value added by its further expression is slight. Everyone knows it, and everyone repeats it, and nevertheless, when set to race against the compulsions of biology, it is left at the starting gate, choking on the blown dust of its competitors, surrounded by vortices of hot-dog sleeves and torn-up betting slips.

Elizabeth married, at age nineteen and very much against the wishes of her parents (Hugh Trainer, an Episcopal rector, and Claire Faure Trainer, the daughter of a glassworks owner), Ainsley MacEvoy, a semiprofessional fighter and occasional handyman, who must have been quite handsome before his nose was broken, and before his eyes took on the liquid vacuity of a lifelong boozer whose head has been too often struck. Ainsley went away for months at a time, touring the ports of the Gulf Coast, where he had cultivated a minor following, and was known, on that circuit, as the "Scotch Swatter," fighting in the back rooms of taverns and in abandoned warehouses, now and then high school gymnasiums, and once, before a crowd of ten thousand, at the Pan-American Pavilion, City Park, New Orleans—the finest day of his life, he always said, despite his loss, on a technicality, to Ezra Lawson, the "Jupiter of Jackson." The roar of the crowd, and all that, and the fat purse and free drinks. Later, as age diminished

To Annie.

Ripest fruit is soonest rotten,
Love and kisses soon grow old,
Young men's vows are soon forgotten,
Look out Annie don't get sold.
Your Friend.
Elizabeth A. Trainer.

January 17, 1779.

his capacity for the sporting application of violence, or application of sporting violence—whatever—Ainsley worked as a bouncer at Gilroy's, a longshoreman's bar at the foot of Long Wharf, Boston, and was much beloved by its patrons, who by turns teased and flattered him, always to amusing effect as he blushed and stammered. Later still, blind in his left eye and deaf in his cauliflower ears, he lived on church assistance, and then on Elizabeth's inheritances, which were not unsizable. He killed himself by drinking photographic fixative—son Bobby was a hobbyist—following the death of his mother, Irma, in August 1916. Elizabeth lived to ninety-one, wore wool hats even through the most overheated Julys, along with, when they came to the market, plastic hair wraps.

The umbrella is an integral element in the traditional image of an upright gentleman. You know which gentleman I mean: he of the black suit, black tie, bowler hat, winged collar, and, yes, tall umbrella, the tip of which he taps, to a martial rhythm, upon the dew-slick cobblestones of the narrow lane down which he strides, bound for the merchant bank, to sit behind his vast carved mahogany desk, with its golden lamp and gold inkwell and pen, reading the morning papers and morning reports, to inflate and deflate and devalue the Egyptian pound, the Argentine peso, the Turkmen manat, all with the same impulsive instinct an artist applies to the mixing of paints on his palette, to launder the bribes of dukes and senators—or bound instead for the Office of Colonial Affairs, there to divide continents into fractious, noncohesive states, prone to ethnic strife and civil wars, the better to extend their dependence on the established political entities and powers of the West, and the better to make them amenable to the cheap and freewheeling exploitation of their resources by Western business interests. The classic man of affairs, is he: one day to loll atop the bureaucratic heap, warmed by the bodies beneath him, subject to urgent phone calls from presidents and prime ministers, and ever invited to fascinating parties with powerful men whose most casual

[47ᵛ]

To Annie;—

Through all the walks of life.
We all need an Umbrella,
May yours be unheld.
By a handsome young fellow.

Etta Smith

Jan. 11, 1889.

FOR. gEt. ME. NOT.

anecdotes reveal secret histories of the world—the invitations always sent on fine-grained card stock, with subtle embossing, and where servants of ideal formality and obsequiousness takes your coat and hand you all your drinks unbidden. Yet I loathe umbrellas. I do. They are yet another object, like gloves and a hat and sunglasses and reading glasses and watches and rings and credit cards, to leave behind at a restaurant table. Those umbrellas of a size adequate to fully protect one's garments from the rain are too heavy to lift for any length of time—my wrists, you see, are victims of a hereditary condition—and too bulky to keep from brushing against fellow walkers. In hand, unfurled, umbrellas appear imbecilic, the props of middle-class neurotics. Like plastic windbreakers with their hoods pulled tight. Like those rubber-soled, rubber-toed duck-hunting boots worn exclusively by people terrified by firearms. It's best to keep indoors during inclement weather, or to risk no more than the brisk jog from vestibule to waiting car. No: no umbrella, I fear, dear Etta.

To Annie

The flowers that bloom in the,
Spring in Autumn they decay
But the Love I have for you
Annie will never fade away.

Your Sincere Friend
Anna A. Reardon

Jan 17-18889.

Faith   Hope   Charity   love

I believe that Anna A. Reardon of 48r is the same person as Annie Reardon of 22v, though I am unwilling to guarantee it. I have no expertise, beyond my own admittedly superb intuition, in the analysis of handwriting, and employing a specialist is not within the parameters of this project's budget—how I wish it were, reader. Support for the independent researcher, support for the very concept of knowledge for the sake of knowledge, is scarce to nonexistent in modern America—such a barbaric land is ours. Were I my Scandinavian equivalent—Teodor Daði, a fiercely bearded, finely suited gentleman of Gothenburg—the resources at my disposal would be of such immensity, and so freely given, that I should be almost embarrassed to deploy them on a pursuit so rooted in the personal, particularly given that I am, in this scenario, Scandinavian: their blood is rich with a modesty becoming in the proper ratios but crippling when too concentrated. I must, we must, remember that the tulip blooms from the bulb, and that the bulb, buried in dirt, is an ugly knob easily mistaken for a rock or the shell of a walnut. Envision the subsidized bachelor's flat, with its clean lines and smooth blonde woods and well-stoked, fragrant fire. The crispbread with lingonberry jam, and herring in gravy, and torvmossa tea, served in the free canteens, open to all, of the aca-

To Jamie

The flowers that bloom in the
Spring in Autumn they decay
But the Love I have for you
Annie Will never fade away.
  Your Sincere Friend
  Anna A. Reardon
Jan 17/1889

demic libraries, open to all, on the elegant campuses, open to all. The energetic pills provided gratis by apple-cheeked physicians, and the injections by their pert nurses in their flattering costumes. The assurance of a publication not subsidized by the author. Modest wishes, and not costly, should a society accept that not all value is tangible, or calculable.

Meanwhile, in America, Theodore Dawes (lightly bearded, suits still fine) is a suspect specimen. Everyone wonders what psychiatric deformity afflicts a person who rejects conventional employment, and unconventional employment, in favor of a life of the mind. Surely he's "had a breakdown," as they say, surely he's "cracked up," if they say that still, surely he's a mere "ass laden with books," as my father says.

No. He's a man dressing himself in the dignity that is a healthier society's national costume.

To Annie,—

Some write for pleasure,
Some write for fame,
I write simply
To sign my name.

Mabel Dixey

Feb. 8, 1889.

"Dixey" is an uncommon surname: a bit of Middle English business, from Dicgsby, meaning, more or less, "Dick's Son." Adam Dicgsby, a Yorkshire landowner, was fined by Hugh de Stanes, justice-in-eyre, for the theft of his tenant's fertile sow, 1208; the Dicsies sat at Sardleigh House, near Tadcaster, at least from the 1360s, if we believe the shire poll tax records, and I see no reason why we should trouble ourselves not to; Clement Dixey, first of that spelling, appears in a parish record at St. Alphege, Harrogate, in 1542, on the occasion of his daughter Anne's marriage to Thomas Wiecker, the rector's son; George Dixey came to Boston in 1750 and made a killing in molasses and rum. In Mabel's case, however, "Dixey" is derived from her marginally literate great-grandfather, an apple farmer of Bolton, MA, who spelled out phonetically his dialect-wrecked pronunciation of the far more commonplace "Dixon" on deeds, census documents, birth certificates, etc.

I, too, write for neither pleasure nor fame. I write for glory, and in defiance of death. I am an erector of monoliths and a builder of barrows. I seat the corpses of kings upright on replica thrones, I wrap their hands around the hilts of favorite swords and insert jewels in the dry sockets of their eyes, I draw curses on the floor before them, I cast spells upon the entryways, and seal them against eternity. Which

To Annie,—

Some write for pleasure,
Some write for fame,
I write simply
To sign my name.

Mabel Dixey.

Feb. 8, 1889.

is to say, reader, that I do write merely to sign my name, on whatever corner of the world's tattered canvas I can pinch in my well-chewed fingers, in weak pigments sure to bleed and to fade when exposed to sun, rain, wind, years, all of which are, as you know, unrelenting. Mabel is more perceptive than we assumed. Good girl, Mabel. This adds no body to her lusterless hair, or flesh to her flat chest, or sufficient acuity to her hyperopic eyes to spare her wearing eyeglasses with lenses as dense as the base of a tumbler; nor does it straighten her genu valgum, or fill the gap between her front teeth, or clear her flesh of its blemishes, which were abundant, and resembled, from a distance, an outbreak measles or pox. We wouldn't want to marry her, reader. But we would enjoy our chats at Sunday lunch, and perhaps engage in a fulfilling correspondence about new books and the news of the day. She would smile at our weddings, reader, and gift us with hand-carved chess sets, even though our brides are unfamiliar with the rules of the game, and are not interested in learning. We would be somber at her wake, and ensure that, at the church, the pews are well-populated.

[49r]

Your Schoolmate.
Annie E. Broderick.
Boston Mass.
Jan, 16. 1889.

For
Get
Me
Not

I rather seriously dated, for a span of my younger years, a girl with the surname Broderick, who I believe shares ancestry with Annie B.—she may have even been a descendant, direct or indirect. This was in New York City, and she had grown up in Rye, but her paternal grandparents, and many generations of their predecessors, had been Bostonian, and were of just the right set for it to feel plausible, even likely. Ms. Broderick—an aspiring actress, songstress, novelist, and mythmaker—and I lived in a two-bedroom railroad apartment on Tompkins Square Park, at a time when vagrants with syringes dangling from their forearms still outnumbered, just barely, Polish nannies pushing the sorts of prams that qualify for auto loans. Together we pursued the louche lifestyle required of young people afflicted by creative pretensions. We dined with men who wore makeup and their girlfriends with serrated haircuts, none of whom exercised silverware discipline or employed public language; somehow the check was always mine to pick up. We consumed drugs, conventional and recondite, in the grotty toilets of grotty clubs in which skeletal children danced to synthesized flatulence broadcast at two hundred decibels. We visited and pretended to admire art installations in derelict warehouses, in sectors of Brooklyn so remote that they abutted the Azores. I found it all quite dreadful, to be honest—I don't like parties, I don't like people,

I don't like conspicuous oddness, and I heard much whispered snidery about my blazers and my loafers—but I accepted it as formative, and knew that much interview material was being generated, should anyone ever write an oral history of which I am a, or the, subject, and Ms. Broderick made lively company. Our relationship ended when I moved to Los Angeles on a screenwriting lark (of which nothing ever came, if you're wondering, reader, though I am pleased to make my most recent draft of *The Unspeakable Menace from Beyond the Beyond*—a Lovecraftian space thriller in three acts—available to any curious agency); I soon met my first wife, whose sunnier disposition briefly invigorated me, and I moved on to modes of existence more dignified, though in the end no less displeasing. Ms. Broderick afterward dated a bass player who was, distressingly, more handsome than me, and she published some short fiction that neither dwelled on our time together nor reflected the correctives I had endeavored to impose upon her literary taste. She died in her thirties—Valium, Vicodin, and vodka, however alliterative, make a reckless mix. My instinct has been to conceal Ms. Broderick's first name—I do hold privacy in high regard—but as she's dead, I don't imagine it matters. It was Ernestine. A pretty girl, was Ernestine: a fun and pretty girl. Oh, well.

There was no need for a telegraph. By the time Annie birthed her first and only—August 17, 1908—telephones were ubiquitous enough in urban and suburban homes that, if a friend could not be called directly, then a message could be left with a sympathetic neighbor. She had, by then, fallen out of touch with many old friends, as often happens when we age, and as happens even oftener when one half of the friendship is emotionally glacial. Annie disliked the implications of a newborn—that she had subjected herself to sexual intercourse, perhaps even willingly, and that, at various points in the day, she must unseal her breasts from their layers of fabric and flattening undercarriage, and expose their flesh to human eyes, however young, and permit their physical manipulation. As many hours as could be managed were spent indoors until young Thomas Dawes had aged to a point where his figure ceased to turn sordid motors in others' minds. Five years of age, or so. Backyard activities were at this point safe, and strolls to the public park, and the greengrocer and the baker, though the drugstore was off-limits, as the boy behind the soda counter—long-armed, black-haired beneath his paper hat, with pubic wisps upon his lip—had a leering, desperate aspect that made Annie's teeth chatter.

Jan 14. 1889.

To Annie

When you are married
And have a little cryer
Please send me word
By the telegraph wire

Yours Truly
Alice M Reynolds.

Boston Mass

Alice Reynolds married Joshua Boyle, her second cousin, in 1894, and relocated with him to Macowan, New York, where he had taken a clerical position with the Tallowmere Company, a manufacturer of industrial steel screening. Macowan is equidistant between Ithaca and Albany, which is to say, equally far from each, and I would not find myself giddy at the prospect of a long weekend in either municipality. Still, ever a slave to duty, I visited, risking bedbugs at a Good Nite Inn, and strep and staph and salmonella at the adjacent Bob Evans, and found that Alice and Joshua's old home, a farmhouse, certified deleaded, with white clapboards framed by conically trimmed tulip poplars, within walking distance to the old brick downtown—the latter a bit derelict, and with three more Christian bookstores, and one fewer wine shop, than I prefer—is presently for sale. The price is appallingly slight, for those of us used to metropolitan real estate markets, though the seller's disclosures, which suggest the necessity of a termite tenting, and the presence of dry rot in the loft, must be considered; and I would certainly wish to refinish the floors, stained by water and gouged by the claws of hounds, and to replace the toy kitchen with colossi of marble and burnished steel. And yet I can almost imagine a life—I can accept, almost, visions of lives.

[50r]

Gertrude Mansfield

Your Friend and Schoolmate

March 1[?] 1889.

Gertie Mansfield was a spry thing, energetic and sharp-witted, captainess of the Pickard School's badminton team, and twice winner of its Blackwell Prize for Elocution. She bore some relation, some cousinship, to Senator Mansfield of Montana, who enjoyed a degree of national prominence in the middle part of the twentieth century, and in the pack of hounds nipping at the crimson hind of Nixon's wily fox. After high school Gertie attended Judd Female College in Pattensen, Vermont, where an uncle served as Instructor of Hygiene, taught for three years at an elementary school in Rutland, married her principal, and drowned in the domestic muck that has consumed so many signees of this album, and that has bored yours truly time and again.

Vermont was a place in which I had no interest, of which I had no knowledge or sense, but to which my research drove me, time and again, and by which I was surprised. Exploring the state in pursuit of genealogical data and artifacts, and crossing it a dozen times, between New Hampshire and New York, between Montreal and Massachusetts, I found it an agreeable polity, relative to its neighbors, and would not have minded further cause to tarry. The ruined houses and factories of its faded commercial towns seem absorbed by the local landscape, signifying and creating balance in the manner of Old

Gertrude Mansfield.

Your Friend and Schoolmate

March 1 1889.

World ruins, rather than blighting nature, or serving as sore remind-
ers, like photographs on a widower's dresser that he would prefer to
turn facedown had he the emotional forbearance, of ways of life long
dead. The double-wides and run-down shacks that are the inevitable
accompaniment to the American pastoral are most often screened by
greenery, and seem like signs of modesty rather than impoverishment.
The opioid and methamphetamine problems are discreetly held, like a
WASP's alcoholism, in the privacy of homes, and in the restrooms of
watering holes no one upright would dream to patronize. The roads
are good, considering the winters, and the restaurants bearable, considering the sparse population. Not too many survivalist, racialist, gun
enthusiast, third-way revolutionist wilderness compounds, nor too
many long-hemmed, dry-haired millenarian Christians. Should anyone ever ask me to compile a Tolerability Index of American states, I
expect Vermont to rank in the top quartile, although of course I can
offer no guarantees until I've devised a methodology.

A terribly good girl—she would have to be, with a face like that—Carrie sought to embody Christian charity and Christian vigor. After obtaining her A.B. at Mount Holyoke in 1895, she responded to an advertisement printed in the *Globe* and took a teaching position at Fort Chivington, Wyoming, departing in August on a mission of civilization and uplift.

Winter 1895–96 at Fort Chivington was notably harsh. The first snow fell in mid-October, and a delirious cold—borne on northwesterly gale called a "Yukon Buster" that was typically of periodic occurrence, but seemed, that winter, unceasing—could not be escaped. Horses froze in their paddocks. The fingers of children turned black in their beds. An epidemic of flu broke out among the internees at the fort's Bedlam House, and spread to the wider community; the dead could not be buried, and were laid head-to-toe, stacked like twisted, violet cords of wood, in Old Pete Andersen's barn. Carrie, invoking the stoic impassivity of her upbringing, altered not at all her routine, and added nothing to her wardrobe but a beaver shawl. There was no condition, she supposed, that she could not defy and overcome with gritted teeth and a saint's ecstasy. One December morning, in the gloom of another gray dawn, as Carrie walked the half-mile from

Carrie B. Millett.
Boston.
Mass.

Jan. 10, 1889.

For
Get
Me
Not

her cottage to the schoolhouse, with her satchel of corrected themes, volumes of Boethius and Jeremy Taylor, and lunch of dried apples, she was set upon by a pack of wolves, and killed. Jake Proctor had warned of the animals—looking dead-eyed and emaciated, their pelts in a sickly molt—skulking about his farm, and said that they showed little fear at the report of his rifle. When Carrie was found in a roadside bramble patch later in the day, an estimated third of her body mass was missing, presumably consumed; everywhere were toothmarks and rended tissue, and blood and fur and crystallized saliva. She was the last recorded American of the old frontier to die in a wolf attack. This sort of mildly interesting fact used to be found in every child's encyclopedia, perhaps in a table or on a chart, and could be memorized by precocious lads to deploy at dinner tables in imitation of the banter of middlebrow adults, who, as you know, make a fetish of facts, and are under the violent misapprehension that facts are a fine and fair basis for opinions and decision-making. A Carrie Millet Memorial Elementary School operated at Sage Canyon, Wyoming, until 1996, when depopulation—the bentonite mine was exhausted, I'm afraid—forced its closure.

[51r]

"May you always be happy through life."

Fannie A. Wilcomb.
Franklin School.

Jan 10, 1889.

Ms. Wilcomb displays in her note either a well-honed sense of irony, or an impenetrable oblivion. Annie was never happy—in youth, in flower, in eld. Wires and a goad were required to raise her bitten lips into a smile. Her fists might have been unclenched only by crushing the bones of her hands—grinding them to a powder, perhaps, beneath a millstone wheel. This much should be apparent from prior notes.

What did one such as she have to be unhappy about? Always a comfortable home. Always supplies in the pantry. No obligation to labor. A handsome husband who bought her any book she liked, any dress she liked, any carpet she liked, wallpaper, tapestry, table lamp, buffet, sofa, et cetera. Annie pursued misery with no mind to the corrosive fumes emitted by her struggle, which seared the lungs of her husband and her child, and mutated the genes of subsequent generations. I am meant—not literally, but you must understand by now, reader, the tone I take—to be a prince, like David's Napoleon, astride a black and sweating red-eyed stallion, hilt in hand, plumage tumbling from my tricorne hat, a vast cape unfurled behind me, my retainers afoot hauling twenty-six brace of fresh-shot pheasant. Instead I tie myself up in the bedsheets of unlikely hotels, air conditioner roaring to spite winter's imposition (winter having not petitioned me to permit its

May you always be happy through life.

Fannie A. Wilcomb

Franklin School

June 16, 1889

ascendance), too frightened to have a meal delivered or to check my messages, hoping this day might at last be the day I spend free from episodes of inward collapse—those tortured phantasms of cracked mirrors, laughing faces, and reedy looped carnival songs into which I must so often fall. That I achieve that which I achieve is a testament to the resilience of the old Dawes spark, the old vigor and genius, which peak like the pinnacles of Mayan temples above the jungle chaos that has consumed their attendant complexes. Happy, Fannie, happy: oh, no. Annie McFarlane was ever a miserable bitch.

The Franklin School for Impoverished Youth was a charitable institution at which promising boys and girls from bad neighborhoods were uplifted by their betters, and at which girls of the privileged Pickard School were obliged to tutor. It was emergently closed in 1893 by the State Hygiene Commission after an outbreak of diphtheria, and never reopened. Fannie Wilcomb, star student, married an ironworker and died while giving birth to her eighth daughter.

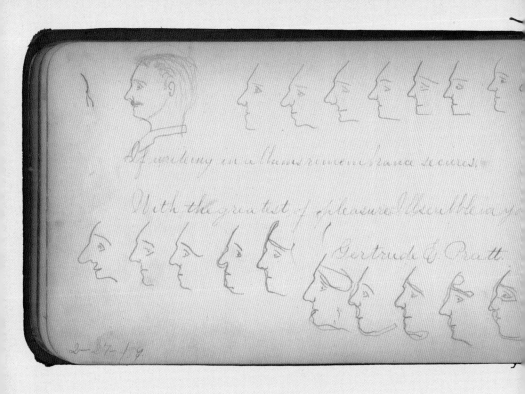

Gertrude, a handsome girl ever adorned in her father's bullion, married Laurent De Meyer, a tweedy gentleman of younger-middle years attached, at the time, to the Belgian consulate in New York. Laurent was fourth cousin to King Leopold, the fact of which neither he nor his wife would hesitate remind all within earshot, should their room not be ready, their soup be served cold, their cab not be waiting at the curb, the price demanded by a street hawker for a sheath of chrysanthemums or a *chausson aux pommes* be too dear. They lived in Brussels, in a fourteen-room flat overlooking Square Ambiorix, while Laurent took on a series of bureaucratic appointments—the sort that took him to the office at ten and returned him home by three, and never left him wanting for invitations to suppers and stays at the finest homes of the countryside. Early in his career Laurent had been dispatched to the Luba Freehold, a vague colonial entity of the African interior, to assist in establishing its gold industry, and in exploration for other valuable minerals, and in the eradication of several nuisance native kingdoms; he developed there a taste for local decorative elements and objets d'art. Laurent led the saying of grace at the supper table while leaning on a lacquered stick, carved with serpentine undulations, that was said to summon rain if struck thrice upon freshly

If writing in albums remembrance secures,
With the greatest of pleasure Ill scribble i nyours.

Gertrude E. Pratt

2-27-/89

turned earth while one faced in each cardinal direction. He wore a dressing gown made of braided grass while he smoked in his study after dessert. Looming everywhere, hanging everywhere, were patterned basket lids, black masks, statues with elongated necks and elephantine ears, beaded portraits, ivory horns, and shrunken heads. As he was otherwise good and sound company, Laurent's oddities were tolerated, and much of his collection now resides in the Anthropological Wing of the Museum of Natural Sciences.

Elder son Major Thomas De Meyer was killed gloriously at the Third Battle of Ypres. Younger son Dr. Mathieu De Meyer, a member of the Belgian Resistance, was beheaded by the Gestapo for his role in the interception of Jewish deportation orders, and in the dissemination of *La Vraie Voix Belge*, an underground newspaper. Great-grandson Nicolas De Meyer is a deputy of the Congress of the Gold Horizon, a national-conservative coalition that seeks the restoration and systemic veneration of traditional social values, a well-ordered collaboration between business, state, and the common man based upon principles of mutual dependence, and the drowning of all Muslims in the North Sea.

To Annie

May your life be long and happy
And your Husband kind + good
But remember it is your duty
For to help him chop the wood

Maggie Mahoney

w Maggie Mahoney

Jan 15th/1889

I doubt that Charles Dawes ever split a log in his life. The Dawes family was of a class that would have purchased wood pre-chopped, and stored it in a recess of their expansive cellar—with the clarets, and the portraits of ancestors fallen out of favor, and the wrought-iron coat of arms, and the bolts of silk, lovely but useless, personally gifted to Abraham Dawes by the Prefect of Shizuoka. A hired man, or robust maid, would have fed their furnace; and by the time Charles was of an age when he might have been ordered by his parents to attend to a woodpile as a ward against weak spirit and ill temperament, a modern coal-fired apparatus had at last been installed. There were few further opportunities, and such opportunities as there were, were avoided. Camping was out: Charles loathed forests and wilderness, and slept in tents only during his military service, over the course of which he expelled much fury in his diaries and in letters over accommodations unfit for a gentleman officer. When compelled to visit one of Andrew McFarlane's "lodges," at Dixville Notch and Lake Mooselookmeguntic, Charles would sulk on the screened porch or in a corner of the great room, curled in an Adirondack chair with a four-day-old newspaper and a late-morning cocktail, even as a shirtless, sixty- or seventy-something Andrew stalked outside with an ax to demonstrate the fully retained splendor of his manhood against a helpless birch

To Annie

May your life be long and happy
And your Husband kind & good
But remember it is your duty
For to help him chop the wood

Jan 15th / 1889   Maggie Mahoney

log. Like assembling townsmen to lynch a thief, like tarring and feathering a predatory customs agent, like stalking and killing one's own supper meat, like sexual congress with one's wife, or sexual congress at all, wood-chopping is the sort of activity one ought to cease when no longer compelled by limited personal means, or the limited development of society and commerce.

Annie wouldn't have helped Charles, anyhow. She had stark, old-fashioned ideas about the division of labor between the sexes, and such weak, spare bones, such a weak, spare musculature, that there was little hope for her to hone for Charles his ax, or to drag it to him, or to get a piece in place for splitting. My wrists are, you know, as narrow as hers—yes, Theodore Dawes, for all his regal bearing, for all his noble presence, possesses McFarlane wrists, or rather, McDonald wrists, the condition having originated with Annie's frail mother. I can fully enclose each one with the opposite hand's thumb and ring finger. They have been the subject of derisive remarks from romantic partners, tennis coaches, bartenders, shopkeepers, flight stewards, custodians, gas attendants, lifeguards, firemen, and sheriff's deputies. I suppose I ought not so often bring them up. I suppose I ought not so often apologize.

To Annie.

"When leisure moments cast a loo[k]
"Upon the pages of this book,
"With anxious words thy thoug[ht]
engage,
"Think of the one who fills this pag[e]
"Your Schoolm[ate]

Ida L Bornstein

Mar. 5 18[0]

An Ida Bornstein is altogether unremembered. Though I have become used, over the course of my researches, to scarcities of documentation, in this case there really is nothing more than this album page. She fails to feature in such records of the Pickard School as still exist, and are accessible to the independent scholar. We find no trace of her in the archives of the state Registry of Vital Records, or those of the Registries of Suffolk, Norfolk, Essex, Middlesex, or Plymouth Counties. There was hardly a Bornstein at all in Massachusetts, in the nineteenth century, which was even less welcoming then than now, beyond the closed circles of scientific academia, to Jews. Puzzling, and I dislike puzzles of all sorts, this sort in particular—almost as particularly as crosswords, and their shopworn logics and punning.

My pet theory? Examine this entry's forced, familiar handwriting, and its too-careful flourishes, the comic pseudonymity of the name: Ida Bornstein is an imaginative figment, the Annie of Annie's dreams. A ghost like steam or smoke hung upon slow air, onto which transparencies might be projected. See now, shifting, drifting, the junior girl academic, progressive in taste and mind, who reads six hundred words per minute, and retains from her reading a mental archive of pithy quotes, which she deploys to immense mirth, shock, and know-

Mar. 5. 1889.

To Annie.

When leisure moments cast a look,
Upon the pages of this book,
With anxious words thy thoughts
engage,
Think of the one who fills this page.

Your Schoolmate.

Ida S Bornstein

---

ing groans—who is demure but exudes a subtle charisma that draws to her clever, sensitive boys—whose graceful dress displays the ample privilege of her wealth and breeding while circumventing, so carefully, pretension and vulgarity—who is bound to climb mountains, cross oceans, take high teas in embassies with Oriental princes and ride elephants in gold barding to their splendid palaces—who will be proud of her husband and children and receive in return their limitless adoration—who is loving, loved, lovable. Dear Ida.

It was a waste of Annie's time, and of her mind's limited capacities, which would have been better occupied by regimens of self-improvement—learning to solve quadratics without the aid of paper, or how an electric motor functions—or by whatever sort of proto-psychoanalytic treatment was available to the common medical consumer as the nineteenth century terminated. This, like so much else, is mere flash, mere noise. No matter the colored lights set to shining, the fog horns a-blast, the cannons fired into the sea, in the end it's just you and nihility. And then just nihility.

Acknowledgments

Although I, like every author worth his words, am the sole person without whom this book would have proved impossible, there are those whose efforts on my behalf, in service and friendship alike, relieved the burden of my labor, and shortened its duration, and for these should be duly thanked. Their order is alphabetical, to avoid hurt feelings.

Ellery Andrew. St. John Balfour. How young your racquet keeps a man. Next year in Wimbledon, eh? Ernest Brigham. Bruce Denman. Jack Dudley. Armand Egleston. Dr. Francis Fannon, internist, Rio Oso Medical Group. I disobeyed my grandfather's firm advice and employed an Irish doctor, who offered a brisk and confident assessment. No cancer. No diabetes. Pre-hypertensive, but nothing that can't be remedied by a regime of vigorous striding, and a dietary tilt toward fish, fowl, fruit. Good health permits the good mind that permits good work. Apropos of nothing *I* brought up, Dr. Fannon suggested prescriptions for lorazepam and paroxetine, and—pending further analysis by a specialist—lamotrigine, a substance most often prescribed to paralyze the insane. I suggested, not so gently, that he ought get himself back to the auld sod, and farm the dirt there, or else I would see him fertilize it here. A brusque blue grape of a man wearing a visored cap on his welded head, wielding a two-way radio as if it were a baton, escorted me to the parking lot. I feel just awful, now. You were only trying, Dr. Fannon, and I am peculiar. My apologies, and my thanks. Chadwick Fitzroy. Paulo Gomes, concierge, Surf Hotel, Tocon del Mar, CA. Towels, ice, reservations, deliveries. I am an ogre before my morning coffee or evening tipple, bearish in the face of disappointment and frustrated desires, and Paolo bore it all with grace and tact. Glenn Hancock. Garry Hoffman. Brian Hurst. Erik von Januschau. *Der Adler flickt seinen gebrochenen Flügel—dann steigt der Adler auf.* Reid Lansford. Leopold Lennox. Upon consideration, Leo, I say, shave it all off. Wendell Mills. Wendell owns Sutton Place's most comfortable guest suite. I suggest his friendship, and resultant hospitality, to all travelers. As ever, accommodating to a fault, you devil, even though I'm a naughty and neglectful houseguest. A check for the broken windowpane is forthcoming. Carney Nichols. Lloyd Pendleton. Cecila Piper, homemaker of Warrentown, RI. Mahjong was indeed a fascinating game, a game of kings, as you insisted, or a game fit for kings. I *am* a king, of sorts, I think. Or a prince. Or, oh, any old royal thing. Tomasz Piwinca, executive chef and owner, Pralnia, Lark Springs, CA. Although we were not formally introduced, I observed him observing my meal from across the dining room, where he lurked by the kitchen door, monitoring service, I suppose, or whatever it is that idle restaurateurs do. We both wore ink-blue suits made with cloths that, at the distance between us, appeared identical. Mine was a Huntsman. We both also wore pale pink shirts with spread collars, and black neckties with half-Windsor knots. I caught Mr. Piwinca's eye and raised to him my fork, on which I had speared a stalk of his ingenious poached rhubarb, and he placed his hand on his heart, as if he passed a soldier's flag-draped casket, and bowed his head with his delightful Continental emphasis. Such are the human moments that spur a man through any trial. Dick Richards. Dear, tolerant Dick. Even when I'm not at my emotional best, you're at yours. I shall reimburse you one day—perhaps a check, perhaps in kind—for the meals, and that dry cleaning. Arthur Carlin Ruggles. Iona Sala, chief housekeeper, Surf Hotel, Tocon del Mar, CA. I aim for an exacting cleanliness in my personal environment, but can't always achieve it, particularly when distracted by stress, melancholy, etc., as I fear I often am. Iona bridged the gap between failure and attainment, and ensured my rooms were ever in right condition for the taxing mental work they were required to host. I still feel a flutter when I recall the bow of her apron string as she bustled about with duster and vacuum. The marmalade *gogoși* she fed me delighted, and the cabbage rolls were tolerable, though cruciferous vegetables create cyclones in my gut; and I still remember, Iona, *unu, doi, trei, patru.* . . . Kirstin Shapiro, freelance copy editrix. She must be the prettiest freelancer in Los Angeles. Her archaic preference for French braids charms, and suggests her rigor. Tracked down the last half-dozen overlooked typos I feared might persist in my work. Wonderful girl. Much recommended. Sebastian Sloane. Honoria Stone. Derek Wallace, barber, The Radical Blade, Tocon del Mar, CA. I require a clean neck and ordered part to ensure an even personal psychology. I had despaired of finding an acceptable haircut without having to drive all the way down to Los Angeles, but was pleased enough by Derek's performance, which was totally agreeable for a nonmetropolitan location. His shop smelled of bay rum and Groom & Clean, and he was not inclined to superfluous conversation. Overfamiliarity is the second-most undesirable trait in a service professional. This is known, but not so well as it should be. Derek knows. Anson Ward. You're a dear friend, a kind friend, and a check for your destroyed pergola will soon be dispatched. Ainsley Williams. Irwin Yancy.

And to all I've forgotten, I pray I am forgiven. On you I promise to bestow bottles of good wine, cocktail hours in the lounges and drawing rooms of our favorite clubs, long suppers in European bistros, fine scarves, ermine wraps, neckties, air miles, long weekends at all-inclusive resorts—all these things in spirit, and for some of you, perhaps, in practice.

Index

funding for scholarly work, comparison of American and Scandinavian, 48r

future, predictions concerning, by author, 46r; by eminent scientist, 36v

genitals, male, in a blood-red sheath, 12v; exhibition to children of, 4r

governesses, untested, 20r

grandmother, toothless and obscurely murmuring, 17v

grave, condominium as a kind of, 10v; exposure of corpse to elements as an alternative to, 16b, 33v; marital bed as a kind of, 12v; marker half-hidden by tall grass, 14r; open, 1r; this project as a kind of, 38v

haircuts, biweekly, 30r; weekly, 7r

halal truck, parked at cemetery gate, 22r

happiness, bitter resistance to, 51r; fleeting and elusive nature of, 21r

heart attack, suffered in classroom, 41r

historians, fat and perspiring, 12r

holidays, unpleasantness of, 3r, 26r

hoop-rolling, as an early sign of homosexuality in boys, 38r

housekeepers, bewitching nature of, 19v; terrified of one's advances, 19v

housing, subsidized, depressing appearance of, 44r

hurricanes, delight in, 10r

hygiene, personal, importance of, 6v, 19v, 38v

ice cream industry, 26v

imagination, a waste of time, 52v

inbreeding, mild and innocuous, 27r; severe, 32r

infertility, male, presumed, 20v

injections, calming, administered by local policeman, 42v

interior decoration, tasteful and restrained, 27r

Irish, the, 1r, 7v, 15r, 18v, 32v

jaw, emphatic female, as a sensual provocation, 19r; weak male, concealed by beard, 20r

Judaism, being mistaken for an adherent of, 8v, 10v

leaves, raked without expectation of payment, 11v; relative merits of those produced by several types of tree, 43r

lily of the valley, unprepossessing appearance of, 35v

lips, anuslike, 1r; thin and purple like a bachelor schoolmaster's, 24r

liver and bacon, eaten at a fateful meeting, 26v

mail slot, unease caused by envelopes issuing through, 7r

marriage, onetime desperation of men to contract, 16v; humiliating failure in proposing, 24r; as a kind of sexual socialism, 22v

measles, contracted from indigents, 24v

medicine, hardly more than a craft, 9v

menace, sexual, detected in low moans and cradled abdomen, 11r; lumberjacks livid with, 13v

messenger boy, sandy-haired, 29r

microgreens, in a twelve-dollar sandwich, 13r

military service, stupidity of, 16v

modernity, Commonwealth of England as fulcrum of, 30r

mole, irregular and growing, 38v; ripe and plumlike, 44r